DAEMON HALL

DAEMON HALL

Andrew Nance

with illustrations by
Coleman Polhemus

HENRY HOLT AND COMPANY

New York

Thanks go out to my idea men, William and James. Your inspirations greatly influenced this book. To my mother and father, who instilled the belief that children can grow up to be whatever they choose. Angie, I'm sure you went cross-eyed checking over the manuscript, so I'm appreciative for the migraines you suffered. Dear JoAnn, your faith and belief are what make it possible.

Henry Holt and Company, LLC
Publishers since 1866
175 Fifth Avenue
New York, New York 10010
www.henryholtchildrensbooks.com

Henry Holt® is a registered trademark of Henry Holt and Company, LLC.
Text copyright © 2007 by Andrew Nance
Illustrations copyright © 2007 by Coleman Polhemus
Distributed in Canada by H. B. Fenn and Company Ltd.

Library of Congress Cataloging-in-Publication Data
Nance, Andrew.
Daemon Hall / Andrew Nance; with illustrations by Coleman Polhemus.—1st ed.
p.   cm.
Summary: Famous horror story writer Ian Tremblin comes to the town of Maplewood to hold a short story writing contest, offering the five finalists the chance to spend what turns out to be a terrifying—and deadly— night with him in a haunted house.
ISBN-13: 978-0-8050-8171-8 / ISBN-10: 0-8050-8171-2
[1. Authors—Fiction.   2. Creative writing—Fiction.   3. Horror stories—Fiction.
4. Horror stories.]   I. Polhemus, Coleman, ill.   II. Title.
PZ7.N143Dae 2007   [Fic]—dc22   2006031044

First edition—2007
Designed by Laurent Linn
Printed in the United States of America on acid-free paper. ∞

3 5 7 9 10 8 6 4 2

In fond memory of Chelsea

DAEMON HALL

Standing 'O' for Tremblin's New Release

BY JOYCE KERNOW, ENTERTAINMENT CRITIC

The King of Teen Scream is back with his latest in phantom fare, entitled *Silver Scream*, and it deserves a standing ovation. This new addition to the Macabre Master collection is part frightfest, part tribute to the horror movie genre, and one hundred percent fun.

Can we expect to see *Silver Scream* on the Silver Screen any time soon?

"Possibly," author Ian Tremblin told me. "At the moment I am in talks with Gilbert Francovich, who did such a wonderful job directing *A Descent into the*

Has Tremblin Gone Too Far?
by BILL BUMBAUER

I'm not normally one to condone censorship, but after reading Ian Tremblin's latest youth-targeted novel, *Necrophobia*, I may revisit the issue. Though the premise is fascinating, the difference between a fear of death and a fear of the dead is not subtle, the disturbing images the book conveys are not for children. Here is a list of the grotesque things that

---

Welcome to Horroronline and our internet chat with author Ian Tremblin

captainq> greetings mr. tremblin. am a longtime fan. I heard the ritual scene from night terrors was based on actual event.

itremblin> Something that occurred near Herefordshire, England, in the late sixties. Mixing drugs with devil worship is never a good idea.

sklyton> it's cool how you go out of your way to meet so many of your fans

itremblin> The relationship between writer and reader is symbiotic; one cannot do without the other.

sklyton> i attended your writing workshop in des moines. do you ever read stories from your fans?

itremblin> By all means, email me your best story.

Horror author, Ian Tremblin, seeks new writers in Maplewood

FROM STAFF

Ian Tremblin, famed author of the Macabre Master series of books for teens, will be in Maplewood next month to conduct a contest to find the best of the next generation of horror authors.

"I have been approached by talented young people over the years who have wonderful ideas for my Macabre Master series," the writer explained. "I always tell them they should write their own stories and take credit for what they create. Now they'll have their chance to get a book published, under their own name, in the Macabre Master series."

Tremblin announced that he is taking entries from young Poe-wannabes and hopeful Stephen King–things through the end of the month. On June 30 Tremblin will arrive to collect all the stories before returning to Tremblin's Lair, his famous mansion in upstate New York.

"There is only one judge for this contest . . . me!" Ian Tremblin stated. "I will choose five finalists. On August 1, the five young writers and I shall ensconce ourselves in Daemon Hall and spend the entire night engaged in telling tales of the horrific. In the morning I will select a winner. The finalists will be judged on their stories and storytelling abilities. I, of course, will be telling tales as well. Any finalists who find they are too frightened to remain in Daemon Hall overnight will forfeit their chance to win."

Daemon Hall, part of the Daemon family estate, was abandoned in the early 1940s after Rudolph Daemon, heir to the Daemon fortune, murdered his entire family. The structure has long been noted in local lore for being haunted.

When asked why he chose Maplewood as the location for his contest, Tremblin answered, "I was born in Maplewood. We moved away when I was thirteen but it was there that I first began to love writing. It seems fitting to return to my roots for this contest. Perhaps I can help a budding Maplewood author find success."

Budding young authors who have the courage to spend the night in a rumored haunted house with Ian Tremblin should turn to page 3D of the Arts and Leisure section for an entry form. □

Prologue

It's going to be a good day. Well, hopefully. Finals are over and I did pretty well. That means I can coast the rest of the week until summer vacation begins. It should be a good day . . . if the fear stays away. But don't think about that. Think about summer and staying up late and sleeping late. There'll be hanging with my friends and watching way too much TV. I might even figure out how to do a backside ollie without falling off my skateboard. I want to enter that contest, so I'll have to do some serious writing. Maybe I'll touch up that spider story I've been working on. Yeah, I think it will be a good day.

Maybe.

I run downstairs in the silent house. My parents already left for work. My brother, Lee, has gone to meet some friends at the pancake house for a before-school breakfast. I'm in a hurry and make a quick meal of toast and plum jelly, pack my book bag, and open the door. The morning sun touches my face and feels great—for a second. Pain hits from nowhere and I grunt. Sometimes it comes on slow, sometimes a little faster. Today it feels like I'm slammed by a speeding tractor-trailer.

The book bag falls from my hand as I clutch my chest. I want to scream, but my teeth are clenched and I can only manage a drawn-out hiss that empties my lungs. I struggle for a deep breath but can only wheeze. A chill sweeps through my body, yet I pour sweat. Dizziness overtakes me and I fall by the front door.

Fear! The terrible fear has returned. But why? Why now? Shaking violently, I crawl into the house and use the banister to pull myself up the stairs. In my room I only think of one thing: finding someplace safe. I crawl under the bed. Fears that never concern me in everyday life now plague me: nuclear war, terrorists, spiders, disease. Then, worst of all, my terror finds focus with my own mortality. Oh, God, I'm going to die here. They won't find my body until the smell of decomposition leads them to check under the bed.

The fear lets up just enough so that I wonder what is wrong with me. One word repeats over and over in my head: *insanity, insanity, insanity.*

Wade Reilly

3318 Cascade Rd.

Maplewood

Dear Wade,

Often when I am corresponding it is for purposes other than pleasure. Most of my mail has to do with business, usually between the Macabre Master publisher and myself. I do spend quite a bit of time answering my legion of fans, but that too has lost its charm. Other correspondences range in mundane topics from research to financial. So it is indeed a great pleasure to put pen to paper, or finger to keyboard, to announce that you are one of five finalists in my young horror writer contest.

I found your entry, "A Countdown to Infestation," promising in its unique delivery of the chronology of the story. Watching the hours tick away for your protagonist and his inevitable fate proved to be truly suspenseful. Keep your fingers crossed that you will win and have a book published in the Macabre Master series.

I will arrive in Maplewood on July 31, but you are to have no contact with me until the following night, when you and four other finalists will meet me at sunset at the front gate leading to Daemon Hall. Please arrive alone. Wear comfortable clothing. Bring a bedroll, though I seriously doubt that anyone will sleep. No backpacks, handbags, or sacks are allowed. If it doesn't fit in your pockets, don't bring it. Cameras, cell phones, iPods, and recording devices of all kinds are prohibited. Flashlights are also on the expressly forbidden list. In fact, anyone discovered with a flashlight will be immediately evicted from Daemon Hall and forfeit any eligibility to win the contest. CANDLES WILL BE OUR SOLE SOURCE OF LIGHT!

Enclosed is a legal waiver absolving me of all responsibility in the case of death, injury, demonic possession, paranormal haunting, werewolf consumption, or vampiric bloodletting. Have a parent sign the form and mail it back to me at your earliest convenience.

I look forward to meeting you, as I am sure you are eager to meet me.

Sincerely,

Ian Tremblin

My brother dropped me at the front gate of Daemon Hall a half hour before sunset. Three others were already there. I climbed out of the old VW Bug and pulled my Boy Scout bedroll after me.

"If you die of fright, I get all your CDs," Lee said, and drove off. Jerk.

I turned to the other finalists. "Hi. What's up?"

"Four little Indians going out to sea, a red herring swallowed one and then there were three," a black guy said. He was about my age, skinny and tall, with dreadlocks hanging to his shoulders.

"Huh?"

"Don't mind Demarius," another finalist, a goth, said. She wore the appropriate black clothes and makeup. Other than a few strands left its natural red, her hair had been dyed black. "He's been quoting Agatha Christie since we got here. Drop your bedroll over there with ours."

"I read *Ten Little Indians* again to get in the mood for tonight. You ever read it?"

I added my bedroll to the pile. "Uh, no. I saw the movie once."

"Books are always better. But you know the story. Ten people go to that empty island and start dying according to the poem. Choking, cut up, poisoned—you gotta love it! That's what tonight reminds me of. Wouldn't surprise me if bodies started piling up."

"In Maplewood?" the goth said. "Nothing exciting happens here in the armpit of the world. That mansion may look spooky, but Ian Tremblin wouldn't use it if it were dangerous. The only thing dying tonight is your chance of winning the contest."

"Ooooh, sounds like someone is full of herself," Demarius taunted.

She turned to me. "I'm Chelsea, Chelsea Flynt. You've already met Demarius Keating. And this is Kara Bakshi." She indicated a younger girl.

I shook Chelsea's hand and held out my hand for Kara. She looked at it like it might be a snake in disguise and then briefly grabbed it. Ugh, her palm was clammy.

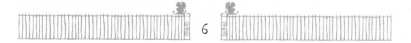

"I'm Wade Reilly."

She mumbled something unintelligible. She was around thirteen, with straight black hair, a dark complexion, and some pudge, courtesy of lingering baby fat. Her eyes were magnified through the thick lenses of her glasses.

"We're all finalists," Chelsea said. "I wrote 'The Babysitter (Revisited).' Kara's entry is 'Too Much TV,' and Demarius," she hooked her thumb in his direction, "has the losing entry, 'The Field Trip.'"

"The losing entry? Someone is living in fantasy land." Demarius rolled his eyes. "What's your story, Wade?"

"I wrote 'A Countdown to Infestation.'"

"Cool title. What's it—"

The roar of a powerful engine interrupted our conversation. A dark blue Firebird raced up the dirt road and lost traction, but the driver regained control without slowing. With a final burst of acceleration, the driver turned the steering wheel and hit the brakes, causing the rear of the car to spin around and come to rest in a shower of dirt. Music thumped but ended as the driver shut off the engine. The door opened, and a muscular guy got out.

"I don't believe it," Chelsea mumbled, and glared at the new arrival.

The driver looked at us. He focused on Chelsea a moment, gave her a wink, and ducked back into the car. He stood again, holding something.

"Here—think fast," he said, and threw it at Demarius.

"Hey!" Demarius held up his arms protectively and a football bounced off his hands.

"Nice catch, Slick," the driver said.

"Yeah, well, that's why Coach Garnett hates me. The only black kid over six feet tall who can't catch a football," Demarius said.

"Coach Garnett—you go to Central. I'm Chris Collins."

Chris stood three inches taller than Demarius. He wore a white football jersey with a blue number five on it. His arms were as muscular as the warriors in the sword-and-sorcery books I liked when I was in middle school. Chris had dark hair cropped close to his head and a fierce look that softened as he smiled.

"Don't pay any attention to Coach Garnett. He's an idiot," Chris said.

"I'm Demarius. I was at the game last year where you intercepted the ball and scored a touchdown. You guys smoked us."

Chris shrugged and turned to Chelsea.

"Exactly what are *you* doing here?" she asked.

"It's a small world, isn't it? I'm a finalist in the contest."

"You lie."

Chris leaned toward Chelsea. "And you still have a chip on your shoulder."

Sensing trouble, I stepped between them. "Uh, I'm Wade Reilly, and this is Kara Bakshi."

Chris ignored me. "Two words for you, sweetheart—*anger management.*" He stalked to his car and got three bottles of water. He twisted the top off one and chugged it down. He stuffed another into a pocket of his jeans and held the third. "We've already started two-a-days. Coach says we gotta stay hydrated."

"You can put your bedroll over there with ours." Demarius pointed to the pile.

"Didn't bring one. I'll share Chelsea's." Chris gave her another wink.

Things got quiet as the sun began to set. I grabbed the tall metal bars of the front gate and checked out what would be our home for the night. At a distance Daemon Hall looked like a castle. Turrets rose from stone walls, and gargoyles perched on the roof. The weathered stone blocks turned from gray to yellow to orange to pink, reflecting the hues of the setting sun.

"Creepy," Demarius said when Daemon Hall became no more than a monolithic silhouette against the night sky.

"As dark as it is," Chelsea pointed out, "it'll be even darker inside."

Kara moved closer to me. I could sense how scared she was.

"I can't wait to meet Ian Tremblin," Chelsea said. "I have over twenty of the Macabre Master books."

"Yeah, he writes over the top," Demarius said. "Which book is your favorite?"

"The first of the Wampyr series," Chelsea answered.

"Figures," Chris said. "Vampires and weirdo goth clubs. It's right up your alley."

"I like *Turn of the Wurm* best," Demarius said. "It's high on the splat factor. The whole time I was reading it, I kept checking under my bed."

"*Knight on Earth* is my favorite," I told them.

"Yeah!" Chris said. "I love how that kid kicks all that demon ass!"

"I'm gonna be a famous writer just like him. I'll have a big house, fancy clothes, and fast cars," Demarius said. "Bet he drives up in something like a Viper."

"No way! We're talking the King of Teen Scream, the Macabre Master himself. He'll show up in a chauffeur-driven limo," Chelsea insisted.

"It'd be cool if he drove a hearse," Chris said.

Kara changed the subject with a whisper. "It's—disturbing—here, isn't it?"

"*Five little finalists.*"

The words were spoken softly, and at first I wondered if I was hearing things.

"*Five little finalists waiting at the door. One vanished down a hole and then there were four.*"

"Hey! Who said that?" Demarius called out.

"*Four little finalists plain for all to see. One was dragged into the night and then there were three.*"

"There's only five of us, right?" Chelsea asked, hugging herself.

"Three little finalists made up this hearty crew. One was forced to walk the plank and then there were two."

"That isn't how the poem goes," Demarius shouted.

"Two little finalists, one went on the run—screamed and tripped and broke a neck and then there was one."

"Where are you?" Chris yelled.

"The last little finalist, almost had it won. Poor thing went insane and then there were none."

Kara, near tears, gripped my arm.

"I'm right here, on the other side of the gate." A figure stepped from bushes by the entrance. As he came toward us, he lit a candle in a lantern. "My last match." The candlewick flared, illuminating his face.

"Ian Tremblin," Demarius said, in awe.

"Guilty as charged," the author replied, and gave a little bow.

He unlocked the gate and beckoned us through, holding the lantern to get a look at us and showing himself as well. He was tall and imposing. His gray hair was cut short, but his beard grew to his chest. He kind of resembled Oliver Reed after his transformation in one of my favorite classic movies, *Curse of the Werewolf*. His eyes were as wild as his beard. By candlelight they were black, yet they sparkled, reflecting ambience, the landscape, and the very expressions on our faces. His untamed look was held in check by a pair of scholarly glasses perched on his nose. He further highlighted his literary appearance with a tweed jacket, complete with suede patches at the elbows.

Ian Tremblin turned his attention to Kara and lifted the lantern to her face. She looked ready to bolt. "You must be Kara Bakshi, the youngest of our adventurers. Demarius Keating, no doubt. Judging by your knowledge of Agatha Christie, I believe you'll have fun tonight." He moved the lantern from finalist to finalist. "Chelsea Flynt, you are just as I pictured you. Chris Collins. If I ever need a bodyguard I'll offer you the job. Last but not least, Wade Reilly." He stared at me for a few seconds. "We should hurry and get a start to the evening. Grab your bedrolls and let's make our way to Daemon Hall."

We passed through the gates and stepped onto the property. The air smelled of mold and decaying vegetation. Ian Tremblin led our loose-knit group up a massive drive. The mansion rose before us and I became more anxious. It felt as if hands were pressed against my chest, trying to keep me back. The uneasiness turned to mild panic, and I finally admitted to myself that an attack was starting.

"Not now." I fell behind and concentrated. "Not now, not now, not now," I chanted, until my respiration and heartbeat began a return to normal. With a sigh of relief, I hurried to catch up with the others.

Ian Tremblin stood before a gargantuan door rising twelve feet high and wide enough for four large men to walk through side by side. Carved bronze framed the mahogany entrance.

He held out his arms. "Welcome, young comrades, to Daemon Hall. At over fifty thousand square feet, it is twenty-five times larger than the average home. I have spent the past day and a half here in preparation. There are seventy-plus rooms. I can't give you an exact number because each time I walked through I counted a different total. It almost seems as if the house adds and subtracts rooms at will. However, we'll only use a portion of Daemon Hall. I have set up our base of operations in a large study connected to a bedroom suite complete with functioning bathroom facilities."

"That's good." Demarius grinned. " 'Because I have a feeling I'm gonna have the you-know-what scared outta me."

Ian Tremblin opened the great door of Daemon Hall, and rusty hinges screeched.

"Man, it's big enough to play football in here," Chris said of the entrance hall, his voice echoing in the vast space.

The murky shapes of columns and furniture lurked out of candle range. Fifty steps brought us to a staircase, marble like the floor, and we went up.

"I'll give those of you who remain throughout the night a tour in the morning," Ian Tremblin promised. "In the daylight it's much less intimidating."

Kara grabbed my hand. I couldn't believe it. I started to pull away, but decided to hold her hand up the staircase. At the top, I gave her a reassuring squeeze and let go.

"Say, Mr. Tremblin, there won't be anybody jumping out at us tonight, will there?" Demarius asked. "I'm not scared, you understand. I just don't like people grabbing at me."

"I wish I could promise that there aren't things waiting for you, but I can't make that guarantee."

"Great, just great. I hate it when people grab at me."

"I assure you that I have not arranged for anyone to do that. As far as I know, we are the only living occupants of Daemon Hall." The writer led us through a maze of hallways, each with a darker and more indistinct wallpaper pattern than the one before. Our trek ended at a closed set of double doors.

"My young protégés, I present to you what we will call the Tremblin Wing of Daemon Hall!" He placed his lantern on the floor and opened both doors, thrusting them wide with a dramatic gesture that left his arms outstretched as he stood, unmoving. The lantern flickered, and the surrounding shadows jumped.

"Uh, Mr. Tremblin," I said.

"Hmm?" Ian Tremblin answered numbly.

"Hello, Mr. Tremblin," Demarius said.

The writer blinked several times.

"Are you okay?" Chelsea asked.

"What? Oh, I'm fine. It's just—I lit all the candles before going to meet you." He stepped in. He walked between two over-stuffed chairs to a big candlestick sitting by a sofa and more chairs. "These candles were burning when I left the room, and now they've been extinguished."

"Maybe the wind blew them out," I said.

"All the windows are closed, as are all the doors leading outside."

Chris examined the candles. "You're wrong, Mr. Tremblin. These candles have never been lit."

We dropped our bedrolls and gathered around the elaborate candlestick.

"See what I mean? The wicks are still coated in wax."

Demarius touched one of the wicks. "Yeah, I think Chris is right."

"Do you know what I think?" Ian Tremblin smiled. "I think this house is going to be a perfect place to tell our stories. Now, why don't you each grab a seat here in the circle? While I *relight* the candles, I'll tell you how we'll go about our evening."

"We know. We're gonna tell scary stories," Demarius said, settling into a brown leather chair. "The scariest one wins. That will be mine, and I get published. Right?"

Ian Tremblin opened the lantern and took out the burning candle. "Not exactly. Tonight we have a format to follow. I came up with the idea while researching Indian tribes for a book I hope to write. In the 1700s, a unique tribe formed in Florida called the Seminoles. It was made up of Native Americans from other tribes, runaway slaves, and, after 1821, European settlers who didn't like the fact that Florida had become a United States territory. In the 1830s, Seminole warriors were led into battle against American troops by their general, Osceola."

Ian Tremblin used the candle to light others on the strange candlestick. It stood over five feet tall and was made of metal and Mexican pottery. The top, where the candles rested, was a thick

metal bar that had been hammered into a crude S shape. The S was not quite horizontal, rising in a slant so that the candles were higher the farther back they were mounted. The potteries were pieces that had been impaled by four metal bars that supported the S and joined together at the thick metal base. Though there were a number of potteries, at least a dozen, each piece represented one of three things: a skull, a skeleton, or a casket.

"Osceola was a thorn in the side of the U.S. military. There was great celebration when they captured him. He was imprisoned at Fort Marion in St. Augustine, where he developed a cough and low-grade fever. A town doctor, Frederick Weedon, treated him. Dr. Weedon had Osceola transferred to Fort Moultrie in Charleston, South Carolina, in the hopes that a change of climate would restore his health. It didn't. He died."

The writer added the candle from the lantern to the last space on the candlestick. He sat on the sofa next to Kara. She scooted away from him, but he seemed not to notice.

"Dr. Weedon traveled to Charleston for the funeral. Afterward, the good doctor asked the chaplain if he could spend a few moments alone with the body to say a proper farewell. The chaplain left, and the doctor opened his large leather medical bag and removed a scalpel. He made a deep incision across Osceola's throat. He took out a bone saw, a saw specifically designed for amputation, placed it in the incision, and sawed through Osceola's vertebrae. Once again wielding the scalpel, he cut away the remaining tissue holding the head to the body. He closed the casket and placed the head in his medical bag."

While he spoke, I checked out the room. Ian Tremblin had called it a study, and I could imagine a man of business conducting his affairs here. A large desk sat by a fireplace. Bookcases lined most of the walls, though hardly any books remained. Open double doors on the far wall led to a dark room, probably the bedroom suite and bathroom. It would take a very full bladder to make me leave the candlelight and go in there. The windows were covered with heavy drapes. Animal heads, mounted as trophies, lined the wall. Their marble eyes seemed to stare disapprovingly at our little group.

"Dr. Weedon claimed to be a phrenologist, a scientist who studied the shape of the human skull, and thought that gave him license to perform his mutilation of Osceola. He put the head on display at his office—after he'd preserved it, of course.

"The strangest aspect of this bit of history involves his children. He was a strict disciplinarian, you see. When a son or daughter misbehaved, their punishment was to spend the night locked in their room with the head of Osceola mounted on a bedpost. They were given one candle, and this was particularly cruel, as that one candle would not last the entire night. They knew that at some point it would burn out. I daresay those children spent more time focused on the flickering flame than the head, dreading the moment they would be cast into utter darkness in the company of this gruesome keepsake from a postmortem decapitation." Ian Tremblin smiled before adding, "They said his children were very well behaved indeed."

"Sweet!" Demarius said.

"Very well behaved—" Chris chuckled.

Kara, a miserable expression on her face, sat at the end of the sofa, as far from Ian Tremblin as she could get. I realized I wore a big smile. It would be a night of grisly tales, and Ian Tremblin had kicked it off perfectly.

"That is the inspiration for our evening of snuffed candles and dark stories. There is no electricity to power the lights here in Daemon Hall. You were prohibited from bringing flashlights. All we have are these nine candles held in this rather unique candelabrum I purchased in Mexico during el Dia de los Muertos, the Day of the Dead. After each story is told, a candle will be extinguished. Our ninth tale will be told as the flickering flame of one lone candle holds the darkness at bay. As for the tenth story— well, we will have to face our fears in the dark, just as the children of the good doctor had to do."

Kara hugged her knees. "And if we don't want to do this, if we want to leave?"

"You are free to go. Of course, you'll surrender any chance at winning this once-in-a-lifetime prize. Because most of you did not drive yourselves, I have arranged for my driver to return and remain by the front gate, should you need his services. He can either take you home or provide a cell phone so you may call for a ride. But I truly hope that will not be necessary, Kara. The night is young. Don't run off now."

I don't know why it mattered to me whether she stayed or not. I guess I felt sorry for her. "Stick it out, Kara, at least for a story or two."

Kara looked at me through the thick lenses of her glasses. "Okay."

"Excellent," Ian Tremblin exclaimed. "You will each, at the proper time, read your stories aloud. But first I want to set the tone." The writer reached into an inside jacket pocket and retrieved several sheets of paper that had been folded vertically. "I would like to tell of a young woman who had a chance to visit a house similar to the one we find ourselves in tonight. That house also had a name, the House on Butcher Ridge."

The House on Butcher Ridge

Adventure and romance are the perfect combination. Not only had Alan asked me out, but our first date would be an adventure with his eccentric uncle, Dr. Artemus Holmes. Dr. Holmes was featured on as many tabloid covers as movie stars. *Paranormal plunderer* is one of many terms used to describe him. As anyone who has seen him on television can testify, he calls himself nothing more than an old-fashioned treasure hunter.

Alan's uncle, a psychologist, got into parapsychology as a hobby. When he began to spend more time with his hobby than his practice, he went into the field of ghost studies full time. After years of research, he theorized that almost all ghosts, spirits who have remained here on earth, have done so because there is something from which they do not wish to part. It could be a beloved home or someone they loved. It could even be an object. The ghosts that most interested Dr. Holmes were those that stayed on this plane of existence to be near their wealth. Money, gold, jewelry, and art were the things Dr. Holmes sought in his supernatural investigations, and they were recovered with amazing regularity.

"This will be the most exciting date I've ever been on—I mean, if it is a—well—you know—a date," I blubbered, relieved that Alan couldn't see me blush.

Alan didn't seem to notice. "There's more."

"What?"

"We get to share any loot Uncle Artemus finds."

"You're kidding, right?"

"Uncle Artemus will offer us his standard fee for assistants. He gets ninety percent of what he finds, and we split the remainder."

❦

"Come on. If you're going to assist me, you have to keep up," Dr. Holmes said.

It didn't seem fair. He only carried a small plastic box, while Alan and I were loaded like packhorses.

"That's an electromagnetometer," Alan said, nodding at the box in Dr. Holmes's hand. "It measures the electromagnetic activity in the air and lights up if there's something supernatural nearby."

We stumbled up the steps to the porch. Dr. Holmes turned the doorknob, and we entered a large parlor. Several pieces of sheet-covered furniture took up space. I dropped everything to the floor.

"Do be careful, Wanda. That equipment is very expensive."

"Wendy," I said under my breath.

Alan put an arm around my shoulder. "I know he's a little abrasive, but keep in mind he's a scientist."

Dr. Holmes shut the door. Full moonlight bled in from the windows, providing an eerie glow. "The moonlight will give us adequate illumination, but I do have flashlights if we need them. Let's set up a video recorder in this room. We'll position the rest of the equipment later." Dr. Holmes opened a video camera case while Alan unfolded a tripod.

"What's the story with this house, Uncle Artemus?" Alan asked.

"Not a pleasant one. This particular part of Pine Rock Mountain is called Butcher Ridge. In the late eighteen hundreds and early nineteen hundreds, a family by the name of Presnell lived up here and made a living butchering livestock.

"In the nineteen twenties it became a popular tourist destination. Some families came each summer, like the Raffelsons of New York. Carson Raffelson owned a very successful import/export business. In 1941 the Raffelson family, Carson, his wife, Amelia, and their two children, Anthony and JoAnna, moved here. They built this house, the house on Butcher Ridge." Dr. Holmes finished with the video recorder. "Let's have a look around."

"Who's going to operate the camera?" I asked.

"No problem," Alan said. "A motion detector turns it on and off."

Dr. Holmes handed Alan what looked like a toy gun but was actually a digital laser thermometer. He explained how Alan could measure the temperature of a spot up to one hundred feet away. "Look for significant drops in temperature." He handed the electromagnetometer to me. From one of the cases we brought in, he took out a digital camera attached to a fairly good-sized LCD. He explained, "A thermal imager."

I just stared at him blankly.

"It allows me to see things that might otherwise be invisible."

"Oh."

"As you've seen, Carson built his family an enormous home. For himself, Carson built the greenhouse."

"He was into flowers, huh?" Alan asked.

"He cultivated and grew only one type of flora—carnivorous plants."

"Meat-eating plants?" I asked.

"That's right. He was fascinated with these plants and grew all forms: Venus flytraps, butterworts, nepenthes, and pitcher plants. Having an import/export company made it easy to bring in weird and wonderful carnivorous plants from around the world."

"A strange hobby," Alan said.

"Call it an obsession. He built the largest greenhouse on the East Coast and quickly filled it with meat-eating plants. Those plants work by emitting odors to attract insects. The insides of the plants are coated with a sticky substance that holds the insect while the plant slowly closes around it. Over a several-day period, the insect will be digested. An interesting fact is the insects remain alive through much of the process. Afterward, the plant opens again to await its next victim.

"Carson Raffelson spent hours each day in his greenhouse, experimenting with different fertilizers and growing conditions. He crossbred different varieties and created what is to this day probably the largest Venus flytrap, the Carsonius Carnivorous.

"Things turned strange when Mr. Raffelson began to experiment by feeding his plants different types of meat: beef, pork, and chicken. He also tried raccoon, squirrel, and deer. Most people considered Carson Raffelson to be eccentric. It was after his experiments with nontraditional meat that they learned he was actually insane.

"In July of 1947 his wife, Amelia, a very social woman, stopped attending all functions. Carson explained to her friends that she had taken sick and was convalescing with family in New York. The children disappeared next. He said he'd sent them to be with their mother. The sheriff was suspicious and contacted the New York police, who in turn contacted Amelia Raffelson's family. She was not staying with them. The sheriff went to question Carson and found him in the greenhouse, pale and weak. His arms and hands were scored with dozens of self-inflicted lacerations. You see, he

was feeding the plants his own blood. His remaining years were spent in an insane asylum."

"Did they ever find out what happened to his family?" Alan asked.

"Carson kept extensive records of his plant research. There was a file titled 'Alternative Foods and Growth Consequence.' Let me quote from the final journal entry—'I am amazed how well my plants thrive on a strict diet of human meat and innards.'"

I stopped and looked at the walls around me, imagining the horrors that had occurred here. Dr. Holmes and Alan turned into a doorway, and I quickly followed. The room was larger than my entire house. Mahogany bookshelves crammed with thousands of books covered each wall of the library. Moon glow poured through a gigantic picture window set in the west wall. I looked out of it into a long-dead garden. Next to it stood the greenhouse, an astounding construction of glass that stretched far into the distance.

"None of the glass is broken," Alan said. "You'd think the town kids would have thrown rocks through every pane by now."

"Townspeople stay away," Dr. Holmes replied. "It's a haunted house, after all."

"Any other stories about this place?" Alan asked.

"Just one." Dr. Holmes turned to us. "Simply put, people come here and are never seen again."

His comment chilled me like the touch of a cold finger on the back of my neck.

"And you think there's something of value here, Uncle Artemus?"

"Indeed. For several years before he was institutionalized, Carson Raffelson stole and hid valuable items that his company imported. Not all at once, mind you, but a little at a time. He'd take a couple of pieces of jewelry from this shipment, a couple of pieces of art from that one. He oversaw the bookkeeping and covered the paper trail. For the past few months, my accountants have been looking over his company's manifests. Near as we can figure, there are jewels, artwork, and valuables totaling six million dollars unaccounted for. Valuables that I believe are hidden in this house."

I sat down, my mind doing the math. If Dr. Holmes was correct, that would entitle Alan and me to share six hundred thousand dollars. It took a moment to catch my breath.

Over the next two hours, we explored the upper floors and then continued on the first floor. We stopped before three sets of glass doors leading into the greenhouse.

"Let's take a break," Dr. Holmes said, and handed us each a bottle of water from his backpack. "I have a feeling that we'll have our best results out there in the greenhouse."

"Uncle Artemus, why aren't any of your assistants here tonight?"

A full minute passed before he answered, "You two are the only staff I have."

"What about Robert, Emma, and Dr. Falstaff?"

"They are . . . no longer in my employ," Dr. Holmes said, carefully picking his words.

"Why? What happened?"

"We—Robert, Emma, William, and the rest—we had a disagreement. I fired them, one and all."

"What was the disagreement about?" I asked.

"Really, Wanda, that is none of your concern," Dr. Holmes said.

Alan narrowed his eyes. "Are you sure this doesn't concern us? What was the argument about? Did your disagreement have to do with this house?"

Dr. Holmes looked at his nephew and sighed. "The stories about this house are true. People come here and disappear. The sheriff investigates, though I doubt that he's taken more than a dozen steps inside. Nobody is ever found."

"How many?" I asked.

"Over the years, at least eighteen people—not counting Hoarsely and Mendelsson."

"Ivan Hoarsely and Dieter Mendelsson?" Alan asked.

"Yes," Dr. Holmes answered.

Alan explained. "Ivan Hoarsely is a self-proclaimed paranormal investigator. He's a bit of a showman and a con artist, so he's not taken very seriously. But Dr. Mendelsson is a professor in Duke University's parapsychology department. He's world-renowned."

"Hoarsely came here first," Dr. Holmes said. "Six months ago, with three assistants. I'm sure the fool was after the treasure. The last any of them were seen was when they left their hotel to come here. Mendelsson came with two graduate students. I'm sure he would have conducted a serious study, but I heard that even he got a touch of gold fever and planned to look for valuables. They, too, never returned."

"That's why you argued with your staff. They didn't want to come," Alan said.

"Robert felt it would be too dangerous. Emma wanted to spend months studying the house prior to setting foot inside. William wanted to come up with extravagant and expensive contingency plans in the event there were problems."

"What's wrong with that, Dr. Holmes?"

"There wasn't time! With Hoarsely and Mendelsson attempting it, every paranormal crackpot would try to cash in on Carson Raffelson's fortune!"

"So you fired your staff and got us to help. When did you plan to tell us? Or did you?"

"Alan, listen to me. You too, Wanda—"

"It's Wendy!" I shouted. "My name is Wendy!"

"Trust me. There is no danger. This is what I do—I'm good at it. We will leave here tonight with a fortune, ten percent of which will be shared by you two."

Suddenly it was apparent that there was a connection between what was happening and what had gone on before. "Dr. Holmes," I said, "everyone who has come here, including us, is like the insects Mr. Raffelson's plants fed on."

"Now, see here—"

"Think about it," I explained. "This house is like those plants. It lured you here, others too, not with a sweet scent, but with treasure. This house will close on us like one of Mr. Raffelson's flytraps."

There was a sudden bang. I screamed. It was noticeably darker as large shutters smashed against the glass doors and blocked the moonlight. Dr. Holmes tried to open them, but they were unyielding.

He turned and spoke in a whisper. "I can't believe I'm saying this, but I fear you are correct. The trap has been sprung. I suggest we run to the nearest exit."

Yet we stood motionless. Another report sounded when a distant door shut, and I fled. Alan followed close behind me. We lost Dr. Holmes as we dashed heedlessly through Carson Raffelson's home. We ran from one exit to another, but the doors locked themselves. When we tried to open windows, the outside shutters loosened from the house and swung shut.

In the far recesses of the house we heard Dr. Holmes calling.

❧

Alan and I sat in the quickening dark, no longer trying to escape. With each slamming shutter, it got darker, until, unable to see, I reached for Alan but felt only an empty seat. Something approached from the hall. Hands grabbed me by the arms and forced me to my feet. I tried to scream, but fear closed my throat.

I heard a voice, a sweet, wonderful voice. "Come on, Wendy. Let's get out of here."

Alan guided me out of the parlor, down the hall, and into the library. The picture window was uncovered, but as we watched, one of the shutters folded over and slapped into place over half the window.

"Now!" Alan shouted.

He ran at the window, pulling me after him. At the last moment, he let go and leapt. Breaking glass flew into the night. I launched myself through the window and landed on top of Alan in the dead moonlit garden.

"Uncle Artemus!" Alan called. He struggled to his feet, bleeding from cuts on his face and arms. Dr. Holmes appeared in the shattered window. He backed up a step, preparing to jump after us. Before he got the chance, the other shutter crashed closed. Alan ran to the car and got a crowbar from the trunk. We went to each door and window attempting to open them. Dr. Holmes's muffled screams made us that much more frantic in our efforts. When his shrieks abruptly died, we got into the car and drove away.

The house had fed.

Ian Tremblin stood and walked to the candelabrum. He cupped his palm around the lowermost flame and blew it out. Then he turned, and without saying a word, strode into the blackness of the adjoining bedroom suite.

Demarius broke the silence. "Ian Tremblin rocks!"

"Wasn't that awesome?" Chelsea said, in a flood of words. "To have Ian Tremblin *himself* tell the story. My God, I was actually scared!"

"Hey!" I cried, feeling pain. Kara had dug her fingernails into my wrist. I'd been so engrossed with the story that I hadn't even noticed, but now it hurt. "Kara, you're stabbing me!" She looked at me with frightened eyes, not comprehending what I'd said. I grabbed her fingers and eased them open.

"Ouch," Chris said. "I hope you had your rabies shot, kid."

Her fingernails had made crescent-moon grooves in my flesh. Blood pooled in one of them.

"Oh, I am so sorry," Kara said. "I was just—I didn't—I don't—It scared me, the story. I didn't even know I grabbed you."

"It's okay, Kara," I said, gripping my wrist. "Just a little scratch."

Chelsea stood in front of the candles and glanced at Kara. "Not to be nosy, but why are you here if you get freaked so easy?"

"Believe me, I don't want to be here. I don't like this kind of thing. Vampires, ghosts, zombies, they're fine for most kids, but they—they—affect me."

I couldn't tell if she was sincere or just being dramatic. "Affect you? How?"

"If I watch a scary movie or read a horror story, it becomes real to me. One time my brother made me watch this movie about man-eating worms. I couldn't sleep for three days. I thought they would burrow through the floor to get me. I knew they weren't real, but it didn't help. I couldn't sleep. Mother finally took me to the doctor and he gave me sleeping pills.

"Don't laugh, but all that stuff seems so real to me because— I don't know how to put it—well, it just feels like I'm destined to have something horrible happen to me, something having to do with monsters or ghosts or whatever."

"Creepy," Demarius said.

Chris went over to the desk. He emptied another bottle of water and rummaged through the desk drawers. "If that stuff gets to you, why do you write about it?"

"I write all the time, but never horror stories. Normally I write my observations of life, like a journal. I write poems, essays, and the occasional short story of the nonfrightening variety."

"You must have written a scary one to be here," Chelsea said.

"I wrote 'Too Much TV' because I was mad at my jerky brother. Peter sits in front of the TV for hours every day. So I wrote about that leading to something terrible. I showed it to him, and he actually liked it. He went behind my back and entered it in this contest. When I found out I was a finalist, I wanted to turn down the invitation, but Peter got Mother involved. Mother made me come. She thinks tonight will 'help me get over the willies,' as she puts it."

"So you don't even want to be here?" Demarius said in disbelief.

"No, but when Mother makes up her mind, you have to do what she wants."

"Your mom's pushy, huh?" Chris asked.

"Mother is—determined. She wants what she thinks is best for the family, no matter what anyone else thinks."

"What about your father?" Chelsea asked.

"He's there, but Mother is in charge. Peter and I have a little joke about them—Father wears the pants in the family, but Mother tells him which pair to wear."

I could see parents making you go to school or church, but a haunted house? "I can't believe your mother would *make* you come."

"You know those parents who tell their kids to sink or swim and throw them in the deep end? That's Mother."

"We won't let you sink," Chelsea told her.

"Aww, how comforting, Chelsea," Chris said.

"You don't have to worry about that because I'm not staying!"

The poor kid looked like she was ready to burst into tears. I changed the subject. "Did anyone notice similarities between the story Mr. Tremblin told and our situation?"

"Sure, it's like he said." Demarius dropped his voice an octave for a lame impersonation of Ian Tremblin. "It was a house, a house similar to the one we find ourselves in tonight."

Chris laughed. "You sound like a teenage Darth Vader before his voice changed."

"I'm thinking there's a similarity between the people, too," I said.

"Maybe." Chelsea picked at a black-painted fingernail. "You think Alan and Wendy are supposed to be us? Not that we're looking for treasure, per se."

"That makes it even scarier," Kara said, looking from one face to the next.

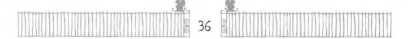

"Why?"

"If Wendy and Alan represent us, then Dr. Holmes must represent Ian Tremblin. He lost control of the situation. And he gravely underestimated the house."

There were a few moments of silence as we pondered what Kara said.

Footsteps caught our attention. Ian Tremblin emerged from the inky darkness and stepped into the light of the candles, wiping his face with a handkerchief. "I splashed a little water on my face. I hope you found my story the slightest bit frightening."

As the writer walked by his chair, Demarius asked, "Did you write 'The House on Butcher Ridge' just for tonight?"

"How insightful of you."

"Is it an allegory for tonight?" Chelsea asked.

"Perhaps."

"We were wondering if Alan and Wendy represented us and what we're hoping to get," Chris said.

"Hmmm," the writer mused, "you mean winning and getting published?"

Chris nodded.

"Would that make you Dr. Holmes, Mr. Tremblin?" I asked.

Ian Tremblin stood in front of the candelabrum. He placed his fingertips together and tented them before his face, hiding a slight smile. Candle flame reflected like miniature sparkles in his black eyes. His smile grew. "I think that the house itself would be a better representation of me."

"The house?" Demarius questioned aloud.

Kara cleared her throat and spoke. "I don't like it here. I'd like to leave."

"I hope you will change your mind, especially since we have not heard your entry. I think it would be rude to accept my challenge and then run off without sharing your story. You don't want to be rude, do you, dear?"

"Of course not," she said. "I just don't want to be here. It was my brother who entered me in this contest and my mother who made me come."

Ian Tremblin stroked his beard. "I'll make you an offer. Stay and share your entry soon. If you still aren't having fun by then, we'll escort you from Daemon Hall."

"When?" Kara asked.

"I'd like Demarius to share his story next, and then we could hear 'Too Much TV.'"

Kara sniffed and looked at Ian Tremblin defiantly. "All right, I'll stay long enough to tell mine. Then I am out of here."

"Are you ready, Mr. Keating?"

"Ready, Mr. Tremblin." Demarius pulled a stack of crinkled papers from his bedroll. By candle glow he began his story, 'The Field Trip.'

The Field Trip

Agatha Montreat shouted at the small children. "I want you to sit there like little cadavers, do you understand?"

She brushed at gray hair that had fallen from the tight bun twisted at the back of her head and rolled up the sleeves of her red flannel shirt. The light turned green, she shoved the gearshift into first, and the bus rolled forward.

A young boy spoke up. "What's a cadaver, Miss Montreat?"

"A cadaver is a corpse, a dead body. Something that sits without making noise!" She smiled at their wide-eyed comprehension.

The elementary run was Agatha's favorite. The kids were easy to intimidate into being perfect passengers. Any trouble usually came from high-schoolers. But Miss Montreat had a secret weapon for when high-schoolers became uncontrollable.

She pulled into Creekside Elementary, and the students filed down the steps in silence. Shannon Glenn sobbed quietly, upset at the thought of being a cadaver.

"I don't know how you do it, Agatha," a balding, potbellied man said through the bus door. "Look at them kids. Quiet as little mouses."

"You have to know how children think, Charlie. Appeal to their inherent goodness."

The man stared dumbly at Agatha. After a moment he laughed loudly. "Oh, you're a hoot, Agatha. You had me going there. Inherent goodness, oh, that's a good one."

"Actually, you and I both know what it takes to run a smooth ship—an iron fist and a swift kick." She gazed at Charlie until he began to fidget.

"Yeah, well, Agatha, I gotta run. Gotta go pick up those savages on the middle school run. Makes me wish we *could* give 'em a swift kick."

"Oh, you can, Charlie. You can," Agatha muttered as he walked to his bus.

Her middle school run was uneventful, though she had trouble from Kevin Mars, a six-foot eighth-grader who got a little bolder with each inch he grew. Twice on the ride to school he called her Miss Man-treat, earning muffled giggles from the bus. She'd make him stay on the bus later in the week and give him an old-fashioned one-on-one Agatha Montreat session. She should have been a judge, she thought. There'd be far less crime in the world with more disciplinarians like her.

Her first high school pickup was at Patterson Avenue and Hobbs Road. Agatha switched on the flashing red lights and stopped. Steve Ritenhour and Bobby Waylon, one after the other, stomped noisily up the steps, grinning at Agatha.

"Stop that!" Agatha ordered. "You will conduct yourselves quietly and not come charging up the steps like a herd of elephants!"

Theresa Goodholt and Devon Ettinger followed, tramping even harder. Agatha Montreat was speechless with rage. Four others banged and clomped up the steps, even little Deborah Raddicker, the most quiet student on her high school run. A conspiracy, Agatha realized. Her face flushed with rage. *A conspiracy!*

Laughing, the students sat and looked at their driver. Their giggles died when they saw Miss Montreat's reflection in the mirror. Angry eyes peered through narrowed lids. Her lips bent into a scowl. What scared them most, however, was when her face, still tense, twisted into a smile. No one spoke through the next two stops. When the initial passengers decided Miss Montreat wouldn't flog them, they bragged about yanking her chain. The noise grew and reached deafening levels. Still, Agatha smiled and drove.

Each morning she drove the bus past Old Warehouse Road and traveled another mile to Baker High. This morning, however, the bus slowed as it approached Old Warehouse Road, the right turn signal flashing.

"Hey, Montreat! Forget how to get to school?" Brian Vincent shouted.

The grinning driver shifted up to second and navigated the deteriorating road.

"Miss Montreat, we'll be late," Denise Wilson called out.

"Oh, you'll be late." Agatha laughed. "You could be a little late—or forever late!"

Agatha slammed on the brakes, sending books, book bags, and papers skittering up toward the front of the bus. A freshman yelped in pain as his mouth banged into the seat in front of him. Shifting into first, Agatha set the parking brake and shut off the bus. She reached under the driver's seat, pulling out a bicycle chain and lock. She marched to the rear, and in one quick, practiced movement, wrapped the chain around both the frame of the last seat and the emergency exit handle, snapping the lock in place. *Snick.*

"I'm going to tell a story," she announced, returning to the front, "and we're not leaving until I finish. If I ask a question I want an answer, or we stay right here until I get one. Is that understood?"

There was no response. Silence stretched until a voice answered, "Yes, ma'am."

Smiling, Agatha said, "Every morning during homeroom, something travels past the school, doesn't it? What travels past the school every morning at eight thirty-four?"

"A train."

"And where are we right now?"

"Old Warehouse Road," Tyler French answered.

"A little more specific, if you please."

"Parked on the railroad tracks on Old Warehouse Road," Todd Bookmeyer said.

Students peered out. The tracks ran toward the high school from under the left side of the bus. To the right, the tracks were only visible for a hundred yards before they curved and disappeared into the woods.

"According to my watch"—Agatha glanced at her left wrist—"that gives us only ten minutes until the train rounds that curve and travels over the tracks we're parked on."

Agatha pulled the keys from the ignition. She opened the doors, tossed them out, and closed the doors. "When I reach the end of my story I will pick up the keys and drive you to school—if we have enough time." Agatha let that thought hang.

"I've been a bus driver since before you were born. Kids have always been the same. Troublemakers. I could always count on the high-schoolers to get full of themselves and act up. At first I couldn't control them. I suspended them from the bus or reported them at the office, but that didn't get the results I desired. Finally, I had a wonderful idea. I drove a busload of smart-mouthed rowdies to this very spot and threw the keys from the bus. I didn't say a word. They continued their loud behavior until someone figured out we were on the railroad tracks. Like you, they knew when the train would go by. At eight twenty-seven they got worried and begged me to drive off the tracks. I told them I would when each and every one of them apologized. They did, and I got my keys and drove off the tracks just as the train rounded the curve. They were angels for the rest of the year."

"So you want us to apologize?" Steve Ritenhour asked. "'Cause we're way sorry."

"What I want is for you to learn what happened to another busload of students and understand why you should never, ever cross me."

A number of students looked at their watches. She did the same.

"We have eight minutes. Let's not waste them. Who can tell me what happened to the 1966 Baker High School football team?"

Bobby Waylon answered, "They were all killed when—"

Chelsea screamed.

She tried to jump from her seat but was held in place. A white hand, luminous in the candlelight, gripped her shoulder. She beat at it.

"Get it off! Get it off!" she yelled.

Kara cowered into the sofa while Demarius, clutching the pages of his story, stood by the candles looking confused.

Laughter erupted behind Chelsea's chair. Chris stood and took his hand from her shoulder.

Chelsea leapt up to face him. "You son of a—"

"Oh, chill out, Chelsea. I was only kidding around," Chris said.

"That's exactly why I think you and every other jock are a bunch of jerks! You make my life hell at school. It's no better when I come across one of you outside of school, is it? I figured tonight would be different, but what do I find? You, of all people!"

"If jocks give you a hard time at school, it's only because you ask for it."

"What? You think I want to be tormented day after day by the likes of you?"

"Oh, please. Wearing all that black crap—doing the goth number—it's like painting a big target on your back. What do you expect?"

"I expect to be left alone!"

"Fine!" Chris shouted. "I won't mess with you again, but you can stop lumping me in that jock category. I'm as much an individual as you are."

Ian Tremblin cleared his throat. "As entertaining as your squabble is, can we get back to Demarius's story?"

"Yeah," Demarius said. "Don't spoil the mood."

Chelsea sat. Chris slumped in the chair by me and twisted open his water bottle.

"Please continue, Demarius," the writer said.

Demarius shuffled his papers. "Where was I? Oh, yeah."

Bobby Waylon answered, "They were all killed when—" He stopped. The rising panic level could be felt.

"They were killed when a train hit their school bus," Andrea Newman choked out.

"And it was right here!" Agatha Montreat shouted. "I know, because I was the driver that night!" She smiled yellow teeth. "I drove the team to a game at Tower High. We won, and the team boarded the bus yelling and cheering and making all sorts of noise. The coaches rode in their own cars, so I was the only authority figure. I demanded they be quiet, but they ignored me. They actually sang and danced in the aisle. If it were only morning, I thought, I could give them my railroad treatment, and then I remembered that a train passed by each night around ten thirty. I didn't know the exact time, but I figured I could get it close enough to be effective.

"You should have seen their faces after I chained the emergency exit, tossed out the keys, and explained the situation. As frightened as you are now, it is ten times more terrifying on a dark night. These big-shot football players were sobbing their apologies by ten twenty-six. I stepped off the bus to pick up my keys and the track lit up as the train rounded the curve. I had misjudged the time. On top of that, I was blinded by the light on the train, I couldn't find the keys. I scrambled on my hands and knees, feeling for them. There was an awful screeching as the train locked its brakes. I remember frightened faces looking from the windows. The impact sounded like a bomb. By the time the train stopped, it had pushed what was left of the bus well past the high school."

"Hurry, please hurry," Deborah Raddicker begged, tears on her cheeks.

"Yeah, dude, we get the point," Daniel Owens said.

"Oh, I don't think you get the point, *duuuuude*. Here's what it comes down to. I hold your life in my hands right now—and every time you get on my bus. If any of you tries to report me concerning our little talk today, I'll get you just like I got the football team. Besides, they wouldn't believe you. They think it was a terrible accident. I told them I turned onto the Old Warehouse Road because one of the players had gotten sick and was going to throw up. I told them it was so dark that I didn't even know I had parked on the railroad tracks. They believed me when I said the bus stalled and wouldn't start. They actually called me a hero because I told them I ran toward the train to try and flag it down."

She placed a hand over her heart. "We had a special funeral at Perpetual Rest Cemetery and planted the team together. It was such a lovely service." Grinning, Agatha asked a small boy several rows back, "What time is it, Ryan?"

"Eight th-th-th—eight th-th-thirty-one."

"We better get going. Don't you agree?"

"Yes!" a girl shrieked.

"Please!" a tall boy pleaded.

"Hurry!"

Satisfied, Agatha opened the door. She calmly stepped down and picked up her keys. She glanced at the passengers when she reboarded. Each and every one leaned forward, mouthing quiet encouragements of speed, knuckles white on the seat backs in front of them. Moving as slow as chilled honey, she sat, placed the key in the ignition, and shifted into neutral. The students groaned as she serenely buckled her seat belt.

"Miss Montreat, it just turned eight thirty-three," Daniel Owens said.

"Then we better get going."

Half a minute after she drove the bus off the tracks, the train shot by.

Agatha arrived at the bus garage in a joyful mood, and it lasted until Mr. Waggoner, the bus supervisor, stopped her by the coffee pot, a few sheets of paper clutched in his hand. "Ten minutes late, Agatha! I didn't know what to tell the high school office when they called."

"Don't blame me, Lloyd. The bus just died."

He rubbed his face and looked down at the papers he held. His angry expression relaxed and he smiled. "You're right, Agatha. I'll get the boys right on 169 so it'll run perfectly for your field trip tonight."

"What? A field trip tonight? I told you I don't do nighttime field trips anymore."

"Sorry, Agatha. I've already checked with the other drivers, and nobody wants it. You're the last one in, so it goes to you." He held out the papers, but she wouldn't take them.

"I will not do it," Agatha said through clenched teeth. "When my brother—"

"Your brother is no longer on the school board. He may have saved your butt in the past, but he doesn't have any pull since he retired."

Agatha's face turned from red to purple.

"Very well," she choked out. She took the papers from her boss and scanned them. "Lloyd," she said, "this says I don't pick up the kids until midnight."

"So you better take a nap today, huh?" he said, walking away.

"And there's no place listed for pickup!"

Mr. Waggoner stopped outside his office and said, "Look over the paperwork, Agatha. You pick them up at the address listed. You can find an address, can't you? Then you drive them back to school. It's just a one-way trip. I guess their parents drop them off earlier in the evening."

"At midnight?"

"The paperwork, Agatha, it's all in the paperwork." He shut his office door.

Agatha shifted into third and turned up the heater. She'd had the chills ever since she set off. "I'm probably coming down with something, and it's all Lloyd Waggoner's fault!" Agatha switched on the overhead light and held up a piece of paper. "8314 Carpenter Road. There's nothing out that far on Carpenter except the cemetery."

Mumbling and muttering, she continued on Carpenter Road, checking addresses on mailboxes in front of the few homes located out that far. After passing through a lonely intersection with a flashing yellow light, Agatha slowed, and only then did she realize she had reached the cemetery. It seemed even darker at the graveyard; she could barely see the nearest headstones. The sign read PERPETUAL REST CEMETERY and included the address, 8314.

"Well, I'll be."

The cemetery gates stood open. She parked beside them and peered into the dark graveyard. A group of people stood in shadow twenty yards inside.

"What kind of teacher would bring a group of kids to a cemetery at night? Must be that touchy-feely art teacher bringing them here to do headstone rubbings or some such nonsense." Agatha switched on the flashing lights that signaled a pickup and opened the doors. The throng of students did not move. She went down the steps and shouted at them. "Hey! I don't want to spend all night out here."

They did not move.

"This is Miss Montreat, the bus driver. *Get on the bus!*"

Two of the shadowy figures shifted, but the rest stood still.

Fuming, Agatha marched through the gates. "Where is your teacher?"

The group started to shuffle toward Agatha. "Oh, now you come," she mumbled.

She turned and stalked back, the group of students trailing her. She sniffed. There was a smell of dust and mildewed fabric in the air. At the well-lit bus she looked back, but her passengers moved slowly and were still concealed in darkness. As they got nearer, she could make out strange shapes. They shuffled closer. By the flashing red lights of the bus she saw they had broad shoulders and oversized heads. Closer still. Were they in costumes? Closer.

"Nooo," Agatha hissed. "It can't be."

They wore football uniforms, complete with helmets and shoulder pads.

"This isn't funny!" Agatha called out.

They were close enough so she could see them well. The uniforms were old and dirty. Their faces were fleshless, their arms skeletal.

"Get back. Get away from me!"

Agatha turned and grabbed the bus doors. Something tackled her.

❁

TEN YEARS LATER

Special Agent Crimmins drove his sedan to the police crime tape and shut off the motor. He got out and ducked under the tape and made his way up the steep road into the cemetery. A man in uniform approached him.

"Are you FBI?"

"Special Agent Crimmins."

"I'm Sheriff Daughtry. Thanks for coming."

"What's so important that you couldn't tell me over the phone?" Crimmins asked.

"I could have told you, but you wouldn't have believed me. This way."

They continued to the top of the hill, which gave them a view of the cemetery as well as miles of the surrounding countryside.

"Beautiful view, ain't it?" the sheriff asked.

"I suppose so."

"Too pretty for a boneyard," the sheriff said. "The property has been sold for an upscale housing development. They were digging up the graves and relocating the remains to the new grave-yard when they made a discovery."

"And that is?" Crimmins asked.

"Over there, Special Agent Crimmins"—the sheriff pointed to the far west end—"is where the 1966 Baker High School football team is buried, or is supposed to be."

"They died together?"

"A terrible thing. Their school bus got hit by a train. Killed 'em all. Everybody except the driver. So we buried them together. It seemed like the proper thing to do.

"Two days ago they were digging up that part of the cemetery. Some machinery malfunctioned and dropped a casket that was supposed to contain the body of the quarterback. It broke open. The casket was empty. So we checked—all of 'em are empty."

"How about the other coffins, other bodies?"

"Nope, just the bodies from the team are missing."

They walked down the hill toward the concentration of uniformed men and women and then up a small rise. Without speaking, the sheriff pointed down.

The FBI agent's mouth dropped open. "My God!"

"Those were my exact words, Special Agent Crimmins."

A backhoe operated below them, coughing up plumes of black smoke from its exhaust pipe. A large hole had been dug. In it, at least six feet below ground, was the top of an orange school bus.

"We dug to the top of the windows," Sheriff Daughtry explained. "Didn't want to risk breaking them and have dirt flowing in and contaminating evidence. We decided to dig a path to the door, see what we find before getting the bus out."

Crimmins attempted a question, but it took a few seconds to find his voice. "Tell me, Sheriff. What number is the school bus?"

"Yep, it's number 169."

"Well, I'll be."

"Used to be an FBI case, right?"

"The victim's brother was wealthy, so we thought it was a kidnapping. But no ransom demands were ever made. Never did find the bus or the driver."

"That would be Agatha Montreat."

The backhoe burped a couple of times, and the engine shut down.

"All clear," the machine operator shouted as he climbed from the cab.

Special Agent Crimmins and Sheriff Daughtry quickly made their way to the bus.

"A couple of flashlights here!" Daughtry shouted to the gathering deputies.

The FBI agent and the sheriff pulled open the bus doors and stepped into the gloom. They played their flashlight beams over the interior.

"Mother of God," Sheriff Daughtry muttered.

Skeletons filled the bus. Each seat contained one or two in upright positions. The bones were clothed in tattered and rotting uniforms. Some skulls wore helmets. One skeleton clutched a flat football.

"Look at this." Sheriff Daughtry shone his flashlight at the skeleton in the red flannel shirt in the driver's seat. The skull leaned back. "Like it's looking in the mirror."

Crimmins noted how the jaw of the skull gaped open. "And," he whispered, "whoever it was screamed as they died."

Bravo, Demarius, bravo!" exclaimed Ian Tremblin, standing and giving Demarius a slight bow.

"Yeah, that was great!" I said.

"Man," Chris shook his head and grinned. "You killed off an entire football team. I like it!"

"That's cause for a few more sleepless nights," Kara mumbled.

"Now you see why Demarius is a contender in my contest," Ian Tremblin said. "There's nothing quite as satisfying as a villainous character getting her just deserts. On some level we knew the ultimate fate awaiting Agatha, but we didn't know from where it would come."

Chelsea leaned toward Chris. "I hope you paid attention."

"Whaddya mean?"

"Next time you think about scaring the crap out of me, keep in mind what happened to the bus driver because of the sadistic things she did."

"Sorry, goth girl. Watching you jump three feet makes any outcome worth it."

"We have one candle too many. Demarius, it's your honor." Ian Tremblin pointed to the flickering flames.

Demarius held back his dreadlocks and blew out the lowest burning candle. The one next to it went out as well. "Oops! Sorry, guys. I'll light it again."

Demarius reached for a candle, but in a spit of flame, the second candle relit by itself.

"Huh?" Demarius said.

"Cool," Chris said, staring at the burning candle.

"Maybe it wasn't really out," I guessed.

"Or, it's Daemon Hall's way of telling us not to get ahead of ourselves." Ian Tremblin smiled.

"Or it's Ian Tremblin's trick candles," Chelsea said with a knowing grin.

"You give me too much credit. I have no idea how that just happened."

"Uh-huh," Chelsea said. "I'll stick to thinking that you're responsible and not this big old house."

Ian Tremblin cocked an eyebrow at her and grinned. "Do you know the history of Daemon Hall?"

"I do," Demarius said. "Rudolph Daemon practiced black magic and sacrificed his family during a ceremony."

"Get real," Chris said. "He owed the mob a ton of money, so they came and killed them all in their sleep."

"Nope. It was Rudolph who did the killing. He was a nutcase," I said, repeating what I'd always heard.

Chelsea nodded. "Something about cannibalism."

"That's often the trouble with haunted houses," the writer sighed, "it's hard to get through the fiction to the facts."

"I take it that you know the facts?" Chelsea asked, leaning forward.

Ian Tremblin sat on the couch. "A writer should be a good researcher, and I've spent quite a bit of time researching Daemon Hall. That led me to researching the surrounding property, and that led me to believe that this is much more than a simple haunted house."

"The land is haunted?" Kara whispered.

"I don't really have answers, just the information I gleaned from my research."

"Uh-oh, I feel a story coming on, " Demarius said, smiling.

"No, not a story. Think of it as background for what we will experience tonight. The earliest information I have about the surrounding land comes from the history of the Nanticoke Indians. They lived here for centuries before the Europeans arrived. This

was an area of land that they would not set foot on. They called it Oaskagu, which simply means black or dark.

"In the early seventeen hundreds, a small group of Europeans decided they would take advantage of the Nanticokes' superstition and establish a settlement on this unclaimed land. They'd been here for only a few months when the children disappeared. The settlers went to sleep one night, and in the morning when they woke, all the children, twenty-three of them, were gone from their beds. They had simply disappeared. Fear turned to panic, panic turned to paranoia. Just like the Salem witch trials, the accusations flew and trials were held. People were charged with witchcraft, pedophilia, selling the children into slavery, or simple murder. Executions followed each trial. A population of nearly one hundred was whittled down to fewer than ten in less than a year. The settlement folded."

Kara stood. "I'd like to go now."

"Frightening, I know, Kara." Ian Tremblin grinned. "That's why I decided Daemon Hall would be the ideal setting for our contest.

"Rudolph Daemon was born into affluence. His father partnered with John D. Rockefeller on many business deals. Like his father, Rudolph excelled in business and finance. In 1928 he decided to relocate his family from New York City, and construction of Daemon Hall began a year later. He lost quite a bit during the stock market crash of 1929, but he had a brilliant financial mind and foresaw the Depression. Prior to the collapse of Wall

Street, he sold over half of his stocks and invested in gold and overseas banking. So he had enough money for construction to continue. Daemon Hall was finished in 1933, built on the very heart of the land the Nanticoke once called Oaskagu.

"In 1942, according to the official story, Rudolph Daemon killed his family and then himself. He left no suicide note, no explanation, and no will. Distant relatives battled for years over his fortune, yet none of the Daemon heirs seemed interested in moving into this vast estate. They did, however, set up a trust fund to pay the county property taxes, but that ended in 1968."

"Why?" Kara asked.

"No one knows for sure. The Daemon family is close-mouthed and would only refer me to their attorney. He told me even less. In my research I did find out that in 1967 several members of the family visited Daemon Hall. They were looking into the possibility of turning the estate into some sort of moneymaker—an upscale golf club perhaps or a four-star hotel and spa. Several members of the family from around the country came. Their plan was to spend a single weekend here and discuss the possibilities. They didn't even last the first night.

"They had hired a man and his two sons from town to come out and clear the overgrowth and brush from around the home. Rather than drive back to town after working hard all day, they spent the night in a tent pitched by their pickup truck. They said everything was nice and quiet at first. They didn't hear a peep from inside the mansion until just after midnight. The groundskeeper and his sons claimed they were awakened by screams from inside Daemon Hall. As they watched, the front door flung open and all the Daemons who were there for the weekend ran out in a panic. Some were screaming and all were terrified. They jumped into their cars and fled without a word to the groundskeeper.

"In 1968 the Daemon family donated Daemon Hall and its surrounding land to the county. The county council thought they'd stumbled upon a windfall. Some members envisioned a new home for the historical society and museum. Others thought that a golf course would provide steady revenue. After one of their weekly meetings, the county council, attorney, and several members of the board came out to look at their wonderful new parcel of property. They stayed only an hour. I don't know what happened—they certainly didn't enter it into their minutes—but they dropped all plans for Daemon Hall."

"So it just sits here empty," said Demarius.

"Oh, every decade or so, when people forget what happened before, someone will want to do something with it, but they all change their mind after spending time here. Frankly, I was surprised when the county council agreed to let me use Daemon Hall for our contest. Perhaps they don't know what happened in the past, or think it's just a bunch of rumors. Maybe they feel the publicity gained is worth the risk."

Sitting in the near dark and hearing the history was disturbing. This wasn't some made-up story, but actual accounts of things that took place right where we sat.

Kara took my arm. I felt sorry for the girl but was getting tired of playing big brother. I pulled free and scooted my chair away.

Ian Tremblin noticed. "Kara, it's a shame you suffer from your fear phobia. Wait a minute." He pulled a small notebook from his jacket pocket and wrote for a few seconds. "I like that, a fear phobia, or fear of fear. I must pursue that topic for a future book. Perhaps a sequel to my best-selling *Necrophobia*. As budding writers, you too should keep a notebook for those little inspirations."

"Can I please tell mine so I can leave?" Kara asked.

"Please, get into the spirit, Kara," Ian Tremblin said. "We don't tell our stories so we can leave. We tell them in the spirit of friendship, as well as competition."

"Well then, in the spirit of friendship and competition, may I share my entry?"

"I'll give you that opportunity now," the author said.

Kara stood. "My poem is called 'Too Much TV.'"

"Poem?" Demarius sputtered. "You became a finalist with a poem?"

Ian Tremblin rested his chin on his fingertips. "Is there a problem with that?"

"Well—yeah! No offense, Kara, but what's so scary about a poem?"

"I'm disappointed, Demarius," Tremblin said. "You seem so well-read. Tell me, what was your reaction when the bird spoke that final *nevermore* in 'The Raven'?"

"But that was Edgar Allan Poe," Demarius said.

"What about 'The Highwayman'?" I asked. A copy of that poem, along with illustrations, had been in a book I had when I was a kid. It gave me plenty of nightmares.

Ian Tremblin raised his eyebrows. "Another fine example. Alfred Noyes's classic poem of love, death, and love after death."

"Poems aren't just about flowers, Demarius," Chelsea said. Let's hear Kara's."

"As I said, my poem is entitled 'Too Much TV.' "

Too Much TV

Peter watched too much TV,
or you could say that it watched him.
The jumbo screen, extra big size,
greatly resembled a large glass eye.
Yes, it appeared to be watching him.

Peter would wake just before dawn,
instead of breakfast he'd turn it on.
It sat in the den like a hungry toad,
luring Peter with its mindless load.
Foolish Peter would turn it on.

He'd sit and stare and that was fine,
except that the TV numbed his mind.
He'd watch and watch, both eyes round
mouth gaped open and drool spilt down.
Unaware that it numbed his mind.

His family said, "Turn it off," of course.
But it was an order that they didn't enforce.
They were busy at work (and socially),
his sister studied fervently
so it was an order they didn't enforce.

Before the screen in pajamas dressed,
Peter was noticed less and less.
Immobile, unmoving there at the TV,
he seemed a furniture accessory,
so his family noticed him less.

The time was right for him to be taken
when the TV was sure he'd been forsaken.
It pounced, grabbed Peter, and have no doubt,
Peter's inside it now, looking out.
Inside it, alone, and forsaken.

His sister walks by later that day.

She hears poor Peter sobbing away.

"That TV is loud," she angrily scoffs,

pushes a button, shutting it off.

And Peter is gone away, forever he's gone away.

ⓜarvelous, Kara," Ian Tremblin said. "Demarius, do you still think poems are incapable of intimidation?"

Demarius walked around the circled group. "It's not out-and-out scary. But there's something underneath that kind of puts me on edge."

"Who can give me another reason why the poem works so well?"

"It reminds me of a twisted nursery rhyme," Chris said.

Chelsea snorted.

"No, Chelsea, that's an excellent point. The simplistic style is reminiscent of nursery rhymes. They may have been aimed at children, but look at what was read to us: the three blind mice attacked by a crazed farmer's wife with a butcher knife. 'Ring Around the Rosy' may have had its origins in England's great bubonic plague. 'Ring around the rosy' describes the rash suffered by those who fell ill, 'pocket full of posies' has to do with the practice of stuffing their pockets with sweet-smelling items to block the stench of death. Some scholars believe that 'ashes, ashes' refers to the cremation of bodies, but I have learned that in the original nursery rhyme it was 'a-tishoo, a-tishoo,' the sound of violent sneezes. 'All fall down,' that's self-explanatory, isn't it? When we grew older and moved on to fairy tales, it wasn't much better. A grandmother in a wolf's stomach, witches cooking children, giants grinding up human bones for their bread recipes. A fairy tale connection strikes a chord in all of us."

"That, and the fact that we all probably watch too much TV," Chelsea added.

"How do you feel about the underlying theme of abandonment? Does it make you uneasy that Peter became invisible to his family and eventually forgotten?"

No one answered. I figured our silence was an answer of sorts.

After a moment, Chris spoke. "That would be nice."

"Oh, sure," Chelsea sneered. "Who'd buy you the sports cars if Daddy forgot you?"

"That's not important to me," Chris said. "If you had parents like Kara's mom, you'd understand. Right, Kara?"

Kara's eyes widened. "No. I wouldn't want her to *forget* me."

"Then she's not as bad as you make her out," Chris said. "My dad, though—I wouldn't mind if he forgot I existed."

"Why? Is he strict?" I asked.

"Nah, not like you're talking about. I can stay out all night if I want. I mean, he thinks I'm at a kegger tonight. Even gave me money to buy an extra keg. Dad believes athletes should get out and raise a lot of hell."

"What's the problem with that?" Demarius asked.

"The problem's with football."

"Oh, please," Chelsea muttered.

"Yeah, you think I'm making something out of nothing. But see, Dad was a big-shot player in high school and got a football scholarship to State. Now that I'm in high school, it's like he's trying to relive his glory through me."

"Doesn't sound too bad," Demarius said. "I'm in the middle of five kids. Sometimes I wonder if my old man can even remember my name."

"Chris, you're just ungrateful," Chelsea said.

"What? Look, Dad's pushing me to get a football scholarship—really pushing. You don't know what it's like to be screamed at, yelled at because you had a lousy practice. If I make a mistake during a game, well, let's just say I've earned my share of smacks upside the head. Dad's mantra is *football scholarship, football scholarship.* I can close my eyes and see a clear blue sky with the words *football scholarship* going from one horizon to the other,

cast in gold and reflecting the sun. How sick is that?" Chris stood and walked away from the circle of chairs. "And here's the nasty little secret—I hate football."

Demarius shook his head. "But you're good. You're the best in Maplewood."

"I hate it."

"To not enjoy what you are good at is a terrible thing," Ian Tremblin said. "Let's not dwell on that tonight. The lighting is not quite right. Would you do the honors of extinguishing a candle, Kara?"

She shook her head.

"Allow me." Ian Tremblin leaned over and blew it out. "And then there were six."

"I think this would be a good time to leave," Kara said to no one in particular.

"I have never seen anyone so eager to be off, depart, make tracks as it were," Ian Tremblin said.

"I'm just as eager to hit the road," Chelsea muttered.

"Chelsea? You want to leave?" Demarius asked.

"Really?" Kara asked. "You'll go with me?"

"You're getting Kara's hopes up, Chelsea," Ian Tremblin said. "I don't think leaving Daemon Hall is exactly what Ms. Flynt meant. Is it?"

"No. I like it tonight in Daemon Hall. I like the stories. I like that I have a chance of winning and being published. When I talk about leaving, I mean Maplewood."

Kara sighed.

"What's so bad about Maplewood?" Demarius asked.

"It's boring. There's nothing to do," Chelsea said. "And it changes people."

"I swear, you goths love to whine. If you hate Maplewood so much, why don't you just leave?" Chris said.

"Hello? There's the question of me being a minor. But when I graduate, I am out of here. My freedom will be measured by the miles that separate me from Maplewood. And you can bet that I'll rip off the rearview mirror before I look back."

"Where will you go?" I asked.

"Back to Florida. Where I lived until my father got transferred."

Ian Tremblin pointed a finger at Chelsea. "Ms. Flynt, please go next."

"Excuse me," Kara piped in.

"Hush, Kara," Ian Tremblin said, and turned his attention to the rest of us. "Chelsea's story is taken from an urban legend that was popular several decades ago. I particularly like her experimental writing style. It's a fine example of good versus evil, the sane versus the demented, the innocent against the ferocious."

"Thanks, Mr. Tremblin." Chelsea retrieved a large stack of papers from beside her seat cushion. "I actually need everyone's help with my story."

"Huh?" Demarius looked puzzled.

"Because of the way it's written," Chelsea explained. "If I

read it, it might be confusing. But if everybody reads it, like a script for a readers' theater, it'll work well."

"Hold on," Chris said. "Mr. Tremblin, it doesn't seem fair that we have to help a competitor."

"Hmmm," Ian Tremblin mused. "Read it as a script. Very clever, Chelsea. As I make the rules in our contest, I will rule in Chelsea's favor and we'll all help with the story."

"Great," Chelsea said, and handed out paper-clipped sheets of paper. "I've highlighted your parts on your copies. Some of you will have more than one part, including you, Mr. Tremblin. Wade, here, your character is Candle Jack. Kara, you're Alice in Wonderland, though it's spelled a bit differently than you'd expect. I'll be the protagonist. Demarius and Chris, you handle the rest. If you come across 'lol,' read it as 'laugh out loud,' likewise any smiley face would be said as 'smile.' "

"So some of it takes place online?" I asked.

Chelsea didn't answer, but stood in the candlelight and said, "I call my story 'The Babysitter (Revisited).' "

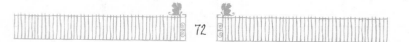

The Babysitter
(Revisited)

creepfan: it was awesome 2night!!!

dungeonkeeper: DON'T LOOK IN THE CLOSET is the best they've ever shown on CREATURE FEATURE!

bbsitter: I just about wet my pants when she went into the basement :)

THElittleRISK: *bbsitter, I'd like to get to know u.*

bbsitter: The kids I'm watching wouldn't go to sleep. I missed the first 20 minutes.

dungeonkeeper: The basement scene rocked!

THElittleRISK: *bbsitter, how about a private chat?*

Alice-n-1drland: I LIKE VAMP FLICKS BETTER THAN THE PSYCHOS

THElittleRISK: *bbsitter, what do u look like? Bet u r hot* ☺

creepfan: i heard they r gonna do a sequel!

Alice-n-1drland: VAMPIRE MOVIES ARE SCARY AND SEXY BOTH :)

bbsitter: The ax scene reminded me of what's going on with The Collector.

Superdude: vampires romantic, alice? since when are monster movies romantic?

bbsitter: Not interested THElittleRISK. Leave me alone or I'll put you on IGNORE!

dungeonkeeper: Good point, bbsitter. Taking the head was a lot like The Collector.

Alice-n-1drland: VAMPIRE MOVIES ARE TOO MAJORLY ROMANTIC! THE HEAD VAMP IS USUALLY A HOTTIE AND THE FEMALE VICTIMS ARE SEDUCED

creepfan: u go bbsitter—put risk on ignore. i'd say his hormones are raging, but he's probably some dirty old man up in duluth getting his jollies!

Superdude: alice, willem dafoe in SHADOW OF THE VAMPIRE was sexy???

dungeonkeeper: LOL. Funny, creep!

THElittleRISK: *don't listen to creep bbsitter. i'm a hottie!*

Alice-n-1drland: THINKING MORE ALONG THE LINES OF BLOND
  VAMP IN BUFFY THE VAMPIRE SLAYER MOVIE—HE CAN GIVE
  ME A HICKEY ANYTIME :)

Private Chat <THElittleRISK>

THElittleRISK: *bbsitter i know u want to have a private
  and sexy chat* ☺
bbsitter: I warned you THElittleJERK. You are now
  officially on ignore.
<bbsitter has ended conversation>

---

dungeonkeeper: A vampire bite isn't a hickey.
creepfan: u r talking about rutger hauer . . . he was great in
  buffy, and Ladyhawke, and the one where he is the hitch-
  hiking psycho killer
bbsitter: littleRISK is now on ignore, suggest everyone else do
  the same.
<THElittleRISK has left the room>
Alice-n-1drland: THAT'S HIM! HE'S A TERRIFICALLY SEXY
  VAMPIRE, BUT THAT ONE WHERE HE KILLED PEOPLE WAS
  TOTALLY DISTURBING
<Superdude has left the room>
<hillstreetKit has joined the room>
dungeonkeeper: That Rutger Hauer movie was called The Hitcher. It's a
  good one.
hillstreetKit: *Hi room.*

creepfan: speaking of vampires, anyone played that new game castle of blood?

Alice-n-1drland: <SIGH>YOU GUYS WOULDN'T RECOGNIZE SEXY IF IT CAME UP AND BIT YOU ON THE NECK (GET IT? BIT YOU ON THE NECK? LOL)

bbsitter: Hi hillstreetKit. I've never seen THE HITCHER dungeonkeeper.

creepfan: that's it, the hitcher! best part is when the hitcher is in a station wagon with a family that gave him a lift . . . he waves at the hero as they drive by and the hero knows the family is doomed

bbsitter: Creep, started playing CASTLE OF BLOOD. I'm stuck, can't move up any levels.

hillstreetKit: *Oh bbsitter, you need to see Hitcher. It's such an inspiration.*

CandleJack: <u>Hi room</u>

bbsitter: Anyone have pictures from THE HITCHER? Maybe I saw it and forgot.

Alice-n-1drland: THOUGHT ABOUT GOING GOTH CAUSE OF HOW MUCH I LIKE VAMPS, BUT THE GOTHS AT MY SCHOOL ARE SO LAME I CHANGED MY MIND

creepfan: hi candlejack, what's up?

bbsitter: Hi Jack.

creepfan: i have the vid box, will scan and send

hillstreetKit: *I have a picture from my favorite scene in The Hitcher.*

CandleJack: <u>What's everyone talking about?</u>

Alice-n-1drland: SOMEONE SHOULD MAKE A MOVIE ABOUT THE COLLECTOR, HE'S MAJOR CRAZY

<hillstreetKit is sending JPEG>

bbsitter: We're talking about a movie called THE HITCHER. I can't remember it.

creepfan: the hitcher candlejack, have you seen?

---

creepfan GIF

---

bbsitter: The Collector would be a good movie Alice. Only have to wait till he gets caught so they have an ending.

hillstreetKit: *How do you know he's crazy, Alice??? What gives you the right to pass judgment on someone you don't even know!?!?!*

dungeonkeeper: Hate to disagree, bbsitter, but it would be better for the movie if he never got caught, more sequels.

bbsitter: Thanks for the GIF creepfan, the vid box looks cool. Don't think I ever saw it.

---

hillstreetKit JPEG

CandleJack: I heard that police think The Collector will try for another head soon

Alice-n-1drland: LOL HILLSTREETKIT—HOW DO I KNOW HE'S CRAZY? HE'S A PSYCHO KILLER . . . DUH HELLO?!?!?

bbsitter: Maybe I won't rent the movie if it's as graphic as the picture hillstreetKit sent . . . looks TOO real.

hillstreetKit: *And how would the police know when he's going on the hunt again? They'll never catch The Collector!*

creepfan: think u made mistake hillstreetkit, the hitcher never had that scene in it

hillstreetKit: *I'M DAMN SERIOUS ALICE-N-DUNDERHEAD! I've made a serious study of serial killers over the years. Most of them are geniuses. We should learn from them, not lock them up!*

creepfan: there are a couple of graphic scenes, but not like your picture

dungeonkeeper: That movie still you sent looks more like a Polaroid snapshot, hillstreetKit.

CandleJack: I heard police studied all of his past killings and found a pattern as to when he hunts . . . mostly psychological type stuff

creepfan: another reason i know it's from the wrong movie is the hitcher never decapitated anyone. the body in your pic is definitely missing its noggin.

CandleJack: Kit, how come you defend someone like Collector? R U a groupie?

dungeonkeeper: You know, Alice, not that I'm siding with hillstreetKit, but legally speaking serial killers aren't insane. If they were, they'd never get sentenced to prison.

Alice-n-1drland: YOU MAY WANT TO TRY ANOTHER CHAT ROOM HILLSTREETKIT . . . SOMETHING LIKE THE GUTTER DWELLERS CHAT!

hillstreetKit: *A GROUPIE??? How can you be so blind as to the art Serial Killers create? And their service to mankind? They rid the world of the weak and they do it with a paintbrush dipped in blood! I thought people in this chat room would have an inkling of understanding, but you are all STUPID!!!*

creepfan: understand where ur coming from dungeonkeeper. but u gotta admit, even though they r not legally insane, they r still as nutty as fruitcakes

dungeonkeeper: Is that the mating cry of the red-breasted North American nutcase or is it just hillstreetKit? Oh wait, they're one and the same!

hillstreetKit: *STUPID, STUPID, STUPID, STUPID, STUPID, STUPID, STUPID, STUPID, STUPID, STUPID!!!!!!!!!!!!!!!!!! !!!!!!!!!!!!!!!!!!!!*

creepfan: hillstreetkit, let me introduce u to my ignore button

bbsitter: Majorly ignore.

Alice-n-1drland: ALREADY ON MY IGNORE . . . WHAT DID I MISS?

dungeonkeeper: El ignoro!

<hillstreetKit has left the room>

creepfan: do u think he was serious?

dungeonkeeper: You missed Kit's meltdown, Alice. We're all STUPID, STUPID, STUPID!

CandleJack: <u>Why would he defend Collector? Guess anyone famous has fans</u>

<LittleTrekish has joined the room>

Alice-n-1drland: HEY GUYS, HOW MANY HEADS HAS THE COLLECTOR TAKEN?

dungeonkeeper: I'm—duh—stoopid—duh—stoopid—duh—what was I sayin'?

LittleTrekish: *What up room?*

creepfan: our beloved psycho can lay claim to 19 heads

Alice-n-1drland: LOL DUNGEONKEEPER

bbsitter: Hi Trekish, we got rid of one crazy and now we're talking about another.

dungeonkeeper: Technically speaking, creepfan, there was a car accident early in the Collector case and two passengers were decapitated. The heads were never found. They think Collector either caused the accident or happened by after the fact and took the heads. So he actually has 21 heads at home in his trophy case.

LittleTrekish: *Hello bbsitter ☺! The Collector is a hot topic in a bunch of chat rooms.*

CandleJack: <u>Good evening, LTrekish. Why aren't you on the Star Trek chat? The ol' Kirk vs. Picard debate is still raging! What kind of Trekkie are you? :)</u>

creepfan: are u sure that story is true d-keeper? I thought it was urban legend

bbsitter: Took the accident victims' heads? That is so sick!

LittleTrekish: *That's TREKKER, CandleJack. Even TREKKERS need a change of pace now and then. If it makes you feel any better, CJ, I am wearing a Federation uniform. Live Long and Prosper ☺*

Alice-n-1drland: THIS TURN OF TOPICS IS REALLY CREEPING ME OUT

CandleJack: I know someone who knows some people in law enforcement. That story about the accident victims is true

LittleTrekish: *It's not an urban legend. Not only did The Collector take their heads, one of the accident victims was still alive when he did. How would you like someone that ruthless stalking you, bbsitter?*

bbsitter: I'm with you Alice, sleep won't come easy tonight.

CandleJack: However scary the guy is, he's only human. The third person he attacked got away

bbsitter: Think I'm gonna leave the room soon. The people I'm babysitting for have a well stocked fridge . . . munchies time.

creepfan: (((((((((((((((awesome info on the collector)))))))))))))))))

dungeonkeeper: The third victim not only got away but stabbed him too. The paper said she sank a butcher knife into his arm and sliced him good. Must have made a nasty scar!

Alice-n-1drland: DITTO BBSITTER, NOTHING LIKE FOOD TO HELP ME CHILL OUT

CandleJack: That's right dungie. She took the knife and opened him up from the biceps to the wrist. Hey Trekish, where did you hear about one of the crash victims being alive? That hasn't been in the news

creepfan: wouldn't that suck? in a big car crash and before u come to, this psycho shows up and lops off ur head

LittleTrekish: *CandleJack, you aren't the only one with inside sources* ☺

```
┌─────────────────────────────────────────────────────┐
│ Private Chat <CandleJack>                             │
├─────────────────────────────────────────────────────┤
│ CandleJack: bbsitter, I need to talk to you privately │
│ bbsitter: No way, Candle. I don't do private chats. Bye. │
│ <bbsitter has ended conversation>                     │
└─────────────────────────────────────────────────────┘
```

LittleTrekish: *It could be worse, creepfan. The Collector is merciless. Let's say he came upon the accident and the driver was dead. And let us surmise that the passenger was not only alive, but conscious and fully aware of what was going on around her. The passenger, hopelessly trapped in the wreckage, could only watch as The Collector took the driver's head. Afterward The Collector made his way to the passenger side. All the woman could do was scream until . . . as the old saying goes . . . the ax fell.*

Alice-n-1drland: THAT'S IT, I'M DONE . . . YOU GUYS ARE WAY TOO SERIOUS OVER THE COLLECTOR—TALK TO YOU TOMORROW NIGHT

dungeonkeeper: Is it true? Was the passenger really alive?

creepfan: what makes u think the conscious passenger was a woman, littletrekish?

CandleJack: You think that's impressive LittleTrekish? How about this? I think The Collector met most of his victims via the internet

bbsitter: Goodnight Alice, I'm about to leave myself.

LittleTrekish: *Alice, hope The Collector isn't waiting under your bed* ☺

<Alice-n-1drland has left the room>

dungeonkeeper: Interesting, Candle. But chat rooms are anonymous. How would he find his prey?

LittleTrekish: *I'm impressed CandleJack. You've obviously spent a lot of time thinking about The Collector. He'd be flattered.*

CandleJack: Finding someone from a chat room isn't impossible. If he logs on over a period of time and selects someone who is a regular, he can learn a lot. Some people say where they live. Some victims may have willingly met him

creepfan: the internet isn't as private as a lot of people think, dungie . . . have read that the alphabet agencies can trace a person through internet use to the region of the country they live in and in some cases even the state and city

bbsitter: creepfan, before I sign off, can you tell me how to get to the third level on CASTLE OF BLOOD?

LittleTrekish: *A few nights in a room, private chat or 2, you'd be amazed how many people are willing to meet. For someone as dynamic as The Collector, it would be like leading sheep to the slaughter.*

CandleJack: By alphabet agencies, you mean the FBI, CIA, NSA. If these agencies can track you down, then why not a skilled hacker? Collector might be a computer genius. It could be a simple thing for him to find out where you live creep, or you d-keeper. Maybe he's been stalking you for weeks, bbsitter, and you don't even know it. Maybe he used his skills to find out you live in Calico Bay, and like a cat with its prey, he's just toying with you

dungeonkeeper: What do you mean DYNAMIC, Trek? You're starting to sound like the serial killer groupie we had in the room earlier.

Private Chat \<bbsitter\>

---

bbsitter: OK CANDLEJACK, WHO ARE YOU AND WHAT IS GOING ON?

CandleJack: <u>Calm down, bbsitter</u>

bbsitter: Calm down? How did you know I live in Calico Bay? I NEVER, and I mean NEVER tell anyone where I live over the internet!

CandleJack: <u>Will explain soon, but right now I need to get back to chat. Whatever you do, don't leave the chat room</u>

bbsitter: What is going on?

CandleJack: <u>Trust me on this . . . please!</u>

\<CandleJack has ended conversation\>

LittleTrekish: *Do you mean to tell me that you've never pondered, in the darkest recesses of your mind, killing someone? Perhaps as revenge or out of anger or merely to get someone out of the way. Maybe you've considered the sweetest murder of all: for the sheer thrill of it! The Collector could be courageous enough to act upon his desires while the rest of you are just too cowardly.*

creepfan: bet I know where ur getting hung up, bbsitter. at end of the second level u will find urself in the castle of blood's library—find the book titled Move me to the end . . . that's what u do, move it to the end of the shelf and that opens a secret passage that leads to level 3

LittleTrekish: *You know quite a bit CandleJack. Why is that, I wonder. Perhaps it's time I leave.*

dungeonkeeper: That's dark, Trekish. Anyone who seriously considers any of that should seek professional help, pronto!

CandleJack: <u>Don't run off Trekish, this is getting interesting</u>

<Little Trekish has left the room>

bbsitter: What did he mean about you looking for someone CandleJack?

creepfan: the ol' creature feature chat room seems to have drawn its share of . . . uh . . . let's say, unique individuals tonight!

dungeonkeeper: This is getting strange. If this were a movie, it would be right about this time that we learn the identity of The Collector. It's not you, is it, CandleJack?

Private Chat <CandleJack>

CandleJack: <u>Can't explain now, but you need to stay on. It is life and death!</u>

bbsitter: I don't trust you. For all I know, you could be The Collector. I should log off.

CandleJack: <u>Don't bbsitter, he'll be back in a minute, I know it</u>

bbsitter: Who will be back in a minute? What are you talking about?

> **CandleJack:** <u>Not now, he'll be back any second. Please</u> <u>stay on!</u>
>
> <CandleJack has ended conversation>

creepfan: yeah, candlejack, ur hobby wouldn't be collecting things would it? like heads! lol

<SlitherKittle has joined the room>

SlitherKittle: *Hello fellow Creature Feature creatures of the night.*

CandleJack: <u>I'm not the boogeyman. You guys need to rein in</u> <u>your imaginations</u>

creepfan: slither, welcome to the chat room of the weird

bbsitter: Hi SlitherKittle.

CandleJack: <u>Hi SlitherKittle, good to hear from you</u>

SlitherKittle: *A babysitter, yum* ☺ *I have fantasies about babysitters.*

creepfan: what brings u to our humble chat room tonight, slither

dungeonkeeper: Hello, Slither Kittle.

bbsitter: Don't start Slither. I'll put you on ignore like I've done with every other hormonal jerk tonight.

SlitherKittle: *I come because I too am a fan of creature features.*

creepfan: yeah, watch it with bbsitter, she has the quickest ignore this side of the mississippi

SlitherKittle: *Don't be scared, bbsitter. I just like those movies about babysitters. The children are upstairs nestled in bed*

and the babysitter is downstairs, all alone. And someone is watching her, she can feel it. Is he outside the house, looking in? Or is he inside, standing just behind her. Are you turning to look, bbsitter?

dungeonkeeper: That girl has lightning-fast ignore!

CandleJack: Are you just a fan, SlitherKittle?

bbsitter: Sorry Slither, I won't turn around to look. I'M TOO BUSY PUTTING YOU ON IGNORE!

SlitherKittle: *I am mainly a fan of movie killers. There's something about stabbings, shootings, impalings, hackings, and mutilations that I find irresistible. From that adorable family in TEXAS CHAINSAW MASSACRE to the body parts gatherer in JEEPERS CREEPERS, I love 'em all!*

Private Chat <CandleJack>

CandleJack: bbsitter, do not put SlitherKittle on ignore!

bbsitter: I've had it, CandleJack. Give me a good reason why I should stay online or I am so out of here.

CandleJack: I'm with the FBI, bbsitter

bbsitter: Why does everyone in chat rooms have to make up stuff about themselves?

CandleJack: I'm a computer specialist for the FBI. I really am. I developed a theory about The Collector that he selects his victims from internet chat rooms. Over the last few months I've spent hundreds of hours online tracking him down and I think . . . I know he's been in this chat room tonight. And bbsitter, he shows an interest in you

bbsitter: WHAT? I mean there have been some creeps online, but I shut them out . . . no, I'm not buying this, I think you're some twisted sicko playing a game.

CandleJack: Think about it bbsitter, THElittleRISK, hillstreetKit, LittleTrekish and SlitherKittle have all been the same person: The Collector!

bbsitter: Where's your proof, Candle?

CandleJack: Look at those names. They're anagrams. Rearrange the letters in them and they all spell the same thing: KILL THE SITTER!

CandleJack: bbsitter, are you still here?

CandleJack: bbsitter, answer me!

CandleJack: DON'T GO OFFLINE, PLEASE!!!

<bbsitter has ended conversation>

creepfan: then u know the movie we were talking about earlier, the hitcher

dungeonkeeper: Careful there, Slither. It's one thing to be a fan and quite another to be obsessed.

SlitherKittle: Yeah, that's a great movie. It's such an inspiration.

CandleJack: It's cool as long as you can separate fantasy from reality

bbsitter: hi guys, i was gone a minute . . . what's up candle? . . . slither?

SlitherKittle: *Reality is what we make it. My reality reflects my passions.*

dungeonkeeper: Glad you're back, bbsitter.

SlitherKittle: *I thought you put me on ignore, bbsitter. Glad you changed your mind. I would have had to end my night earlier than planned.*

CandleJack: *I'm very happy you're still with us bbsitter*

bbsitter: sorry slither, sometimes I get a little worried about who's online with me. who knows, you could be the collector :)

Private Chat <CandleJack>

CandleJack: Thank God you stayed online, bbsitter

bbsitter: i'm so scared. what am i supposed to do?

CandleJack: Just keep him online. It's like creepfan said earlier, we alphabet agencies can trace internet users to regions, states, and sometimes even cities. What the general population doesn't know is that with the right software, enough time, and the top computer specialists, we can trace them to their exact computer location. It's the cyber version of a phone trace

bbsitter: you can do this?

CandleJack: I have the program and I'm one of the best. I need you to get me the time

bbsitter: oh god, how long will that take?

CandleJack: I've been working on it all night. Even though he logs off and then comes back with a

---

different name, I'm still tracking him. In fact, I know
what city he's in. Don't panic bbsitter, but he's there
in Calico Bay

CandleJack: bbsitter, are you all right?

CandleJack: bbsitter?

bbsitter: you don't mean that he's just showing an
interest in me. you really mean he's chosen me as his
next victim, right?

CandleJack: He's probably been monitoring you for
months in this room, and using that time to track
you down. Give me your name and the address of
where you're babysitting. If it gets dangerous I'll
have the police there in minutes

bbsitter: my name is jessica brightman, the address
here is 1611 quayside drive.

bbsitter: am i safe, candlejack?

CandleJack: As long as he's in the chat room you know
he's on his computer and not outside your door. Get
back and talk to him. Keep him chatting

bbsitter: i'm so scared. i'll screw it up.

CandleJack: Get him to talk about himself. Killers like
this guy love to talk about themselves

bbsitter: i'll try.

CandleJack: I can't ask for more than that. I'll let you
know when I've pinpointed his location. It shouldn't
be much longer

<CandleJack has ended conversation>

dungeonkeeper: No way, creepfan. Freddie Krueger has Jason beat by a long shot.

creepfan: (((((((((((((jason rules!!!))))))))))))))

bbsitter: so slitherkittle, what do you do for fun?

dungeonkeeper: How many months have we been having this argument, creepy?

Private Chat <SlitherKittle>

SlitherKittle: *For fun? I think a private chat with you would be fun.*

bbsitter: why not? tell me about yourself.

SlitherKittle: *Let's see, what are my qualities? I'm a hot-tie, bbsitter. And I'm a genius. How do I sound so far?*

bbsitter: intriguing, go on.

SlitherKittle: *I'm dynamic. I can be ruthless. Let's not forget courageous.*

bbsitter: or modest :)

SlitherKittle: *Oh please, modesty is a false quality. If you're confident about yourself, modesty is just an air to put on so all the losers around you won't feel inferior. Why?*

bbsitter: good point. so slither, what would you say is your most outstanding trait?

SlitherKittle: *That's easy. I'm MERCILESS!*

SlitherKittle: *Oh bbsitter.*

SlitherKittle: *Are you there bbsitter? Am I scaring you?*

bbsitter: no, i was just thinking about what you've said.

SlitherKittle: *You asked me what I do for fun. Shall I tell you?*

bbsitter: sure.

SlitherKittle: *I like to imagine what people I'm chatting with look like, what they're doing besides pecking on their little keyboards.*

bbsitter: what do you imagine i look like?

SlitherKittle: *I think you look yummy☺! There's a certain helpless quality to babysitters that I find irresistible.*

bbsitter: helpless quality?

SlitherKittle: *Sure. You're charged with protecting two little munchkins from harm while you yourself are not much older than they are.*

bbsitter: how do you know i'm babysitting two kids?

SlitherKittle: *A lucky guess, average American household and all that. As I was saying, you're there alone, supposed to protect the children, but who's going to protect you?*

bbsitter: do i need protecting?

SlitherKittle: *I picture you sitting downstairs at the computer where you're babysitting. Your long blond hair is pulled into a ponytail. How am I doing so far, bbsitter?*

bbsitter: pretty good, slither. should i try you?

SlitherKittle: *Not so fast bbsitter, let me finish. You're wearing lounging clothes, an unbuttoned blue flannel shirt over a pink tank top.*

bbsitter: how do you know that?

SlitherKittle: *Gray sweatpants round out your non-matching ensemble. They're a bit frayed about the ankles.*

bbsitter: where are you?

SlitherKittle: *Your beautiful feet are bare. That plush carpet must feel delicious on your naked feet. Now you're wondering, "Is he peeking through the windows? Did he watch me as I arrived?"*

SlitherKittle: *And now you wonder, "Is he The Collector? Will he take my head and put it in a bowling ball bag to carry home with him?"*

SlitherKittle: *You're thinking, "Will he put my head on the shelf in his basement with the others?"*

bbsitter: STOP!

SlitherKittle: *I must say goodbye to the Creature Feature Chat Room, as I have business to attend to.*

bbsitter: no wait!

bbsitter: don't go yet!

<SlitherKittle has ended conversation>

<SlitherKittle has left the room>

bbsitter: CandleJack, was on a private chat with slitherkittle but I lost him. i think he is the collector!

CandleJack: <u>BBSITTER, GET OUT!</u>

bbsitter: what?

CandleJack: <u>LEAVE! GET OUT NOW!</u>

bbsitter: leave the room? why?

CandleJack: <u>NO! GET OUT OF THAT HOUSE!</u>

bbsitter: what are you talking about?

CandleJack: <u>I FINALLY TRACED THE COLLECTOR'S LOCATION!
IT'S 1611 QUAYSIDE DRIVE! HE'S BEEN USING ANOTHER
COMPUTER IN THE HOME WHERE YOU'RE BABYSITTING!!!</u>

$\mathbf{D}$amn," I said, rubbing the goose bumps on my arms. "You ought to focus on scripts and screenplays."

"Definitely!" Demarius agreed. "Even though I was reading as a character, that ending still gave me chills."

"Not bad, goth girl." Chris smiled. "I'll be in your readers' theater any day."

"I hate psycho stories. They scare me more than all the others," Kara said miserably.

"That's interesting, Kara," Ian Tremblin said.

"My brother told me the original 'Babysitter' a long time ago," I remembered. "The killer kept calling on the phone until the operator traced the call to an extension in the house. It's a great story, but one thing bothered me. Did the babysitter get away or not?"

"Sometimes it's best to leave your readers hanging," Ian Tremblin offered. "The uncertainty can be as unsettling as the story itself."

"There's something I've been wanting to do all night." Chelsea put her story on a chair and took a step toward the candelabrum. She inhaled in preparation to blow out a candle. One moment all was still; the next, a tremendous wind raged into the study. Chelsea's black hair rose around her head, and the pages of her story blew into the air and kited around the room. "What's going on?" she yelled. She leaned into the windstorm, but it forced her back several steps.

We all stood up, except for Kara, who twisted on the sofa and hid her face. The gale snuffed out the candles and then died. No one moved in the total darkness. Intense pressure filled the room. My ears had that feeling of swimming to the bottom of a deep pool. Then, like an exhalation, the pressure lifted. In the depths of the old house I heard something. We all did.

"It sounds like—like running water," Chris whispered.

Kara came to me, and I put my arm around her, for myself as much as for her. "No," she whispered, "not water. Someone is laughing—crazy laughing."

"You're wrong," Demarius said. "Listen. Something is breaking."

"Snapped," Chelsea whispered.

"You're all wrong," I said. Couldn't they hear it? "Someone is screaming."

Five candles reignited in a sputter of flames and murky light.

Chelsea, hair askew, turned to Ian Tremblin and smiled. "Awesome! How did you do that? Where'd the wind come from? How did the candles light back up? Is there a special effects crew in Daemon Hall trying to scare us?"

"Hmmm." He pulled at his beard, his lips pursed. "That would certainly be the logical explanation."

"It was you, wasn't it?" Kara asked.

"This night just gets better and better." Demarius grinned. "Man, my heart is beating a mile a minute."

Chris exhaled and smiled at me. I tried to return the grin but couldn't. My mind was trying to rationalize why the voice I heard screaming, the voice in the bowels of Daemon Hall, had been my own.

Ian Tremblin stretched and meandered to the candles, where he put a finger thoughtfully to his lips. "I didn't hear a thing, other than the wind. And it's curious how these candles lit up again."

In the wavering glow of five candles, the skeletal potteries looked like they were moving in the candelabrum frame. We all took our seats, and I put a hand on my chest as if I could slow the rapid heartbeats by putting pressure on it.

Demarius cleared his throat. "Hey, Mr. Tremblin, can I ask you a personal question?"

He turned from the candles. "Fire away, young man."

"With all the money you make, how come you don't have more style? Why are you wearing that putzy old jacket? It's kind of cliché for a writer, don't you think?"

Chelsea barked a laugh. "Jeez, Demarius. Like you're Mr. Fashion. Your pants are so loose I expect them to drop to your ankles and reveal the red hearts on your boxers."

Demarius turned on her. "You're one to talk, Miss Vampire Chic/Goodwill Geek. And for your information, it's little Tasmanian devils!"

"What are you talking about?"

"My boxers. It's Taz on my boxers, not hearts!"

"Calm down, you two. I don't mind the question. The reason I wear this jacket goes back to my high school days," Ian Tremblin said, "when I took creative writing under the tutelage of Mr. Ellis Clementine. He wore a jacket like this."

"So, he was an inspiration to you?" I guessed.

"Oh, no. The opposite. Mr. Clementine loved to tell his students that he could've been a published author any time he chose, but preferred the life of an academic. I won't dignify that rubbish with my opinion." Ian Tremblin straightened a candle and turned to face the finalists. "You can probably tell I was not fond of the man. Mr. Clementine was a terrible writing instructor. He praised his pet students and harshly criticized the rest, including me.

"Toward the end of term he assigned us a short story that would count for a quarter of our grade. For three weeks I worked

five hours a night on that story, writing and rewriting, editing and editing again. This was in the days before home computers and printers, so I had the story professionally printed on good-quality paper stock. When I picked it up I was so pleased with how it turned out that I ordered another copy, just in case Mr. Clementine wanted to keep mine to use as a teaching tool.

"After two weeks he returned our stories. Mine did not have a grade, only a note penciled in red that said to meet with him after class. I shook with nervousness as I stood at his desk. 'Mr. Tremblin,' he began, 'as a certified instructor in the creative writing department, it is often my unpleasant task to separate the wheat from the chaff. I know it is your desire to pursue a career in writing, so I hope you'll know I am only saying this as a favor to you. Mr. Tremblin, this story has demonstrated that you have no talent for writing. You will never find success as a professional writer.'

"He went on for some time, but I no longer heard him. I was shell-shocked. I believed that my goal in life would not come to fruition. Not even out of high school and I already felt like a failure. Oh, the bleak thoughts that plagued my mind.

"A week later, I received a call from the printer asking if I was going to pick up the other copy of the story I had ordered. Before I could tell him to throw it out, he informed me that he had read it. 'I hope you don't mind,' he said. 'But that first sentence hooked me, kid. The next thing you know, I'm sitting on a box of paper and reading the whole thing. I couldn't put it down. Everybody in the shop loved it. You know what, kid? You got a bright future ahead of you.'

"That's when I realized that Mr. Clementine might know plenty about grammar, syntax, and sentence structure, but he didn't know a thing about what makes a good story. When my first book was published I bought a tweed jacket just like the one Mr. Clementine wore. It was my little way of gloating.

"Now, I had planned for Mr. Reilly to regale us with his story next. However, Kara has already stated that a certain type of story scares her more than others, and what is one of the reasons we gather tonight? So that we may all have a good scare. That is why I will change the roster and invite Mr. Collins to go next."

"About time." Chris jumped to his feet and pulled folded papers from his back pocket. He moved to the candles and stared at his papers a moment. "You know, it's strange—no, it's probably a coincidence."

"What is, Mr. Collins?"

"I wrote this story after you first announced your contest. I didn't know who would be here tonight, other than you, Mr. Tremblin. Yet it's almost like I drew from our group for my characters."

"How's that?" Demarius asked.

"It's like I used Kara for a character who is where she does not

want to be. And if I didn't know better, I'd say the protagonist is inspired by Chelsea *and* Wade. Wade because he protects the vulnerable. And Chelsea because she is so eager to leave town." Chris closed his eyes, and I wondered if he saw what he spoke of. "He can't stop riding, traveling, putting miles behind him. He rides the black wind."

Ride the Black Wind

Ketch shifted into fourth gear. The roar of his motorcycle dropped a notch and ran at a steady rumble on the desert highway. Gusts blew swirls of sand across the road. Tumbleweeds danced to the silent music of wind.

"Swirling sand and dancing tumbleweeds," Chelsea muttered. "Besides self-proclaimed writer and artist, I guess you're a cowboy poet, too."

Chris ignored her.

This was where he found peace—riding his old motorcycle, Black Wind. It was black with red flames on the tank. He'd painted it himself, and it was a crappy job, but all his money went into keeping the old Harley-Davidson running. No way he could afford a professional paint job.

The freedom he felt flying down the highway could be measured in miles. Each mile symbolized when he would eventually leave his lame hometown, Canyon, Arizona. When he left, he wouldn't look back. He would rip off the rearview mirror before he did that.

"Oh, please!" Chelsea pointed a finger at Chris. "You didn't write that. You just stuck that in there to mess with my head."

Chris didn't respond, he merely looked uneasily at Chelsea. She noticed the rest of us looking at her, puzzled.

"Don't you remember? A little earlier I said I'd leave Maplewood and would rip off the mirror before I looked back. All of a sudden, it shows up in his story. He's being a jerk and trying to freak me out or something."

Chris held out the printed pages to Chelsea, his finger on one particular sentence.

She read a moment, then quietly said, "Oh."

"I told you it was weird, how the characters match up with you and . . ." Chris looked at Kara and me.

"Coincidence or precognition." Ian Tremblin threw up his hands in a dismissive gesture. "Either way, it doesn't affect the story. On with it, Chris."

The only thing Ketch would regret would be leaving his older brother, a biker and carpenter he'd lived with since their parents were killed in a traffic accident.

"What about his friends?"

"Demarius!" Ian Tremblin chided.

"Sorry. I didn't mean to interrupt the story. It's just that— doesn't Ketch have any friends?"

"Nope," Chris said. "People are intimidated by him. A lot of it is how he looks. He has long tangled hair and this ratty-assed goatee. He's usually coated in road dust. You'd approve of his wardrobe, Chelsea—plenty of black leather, including fingerless black gloves. His usual expression is a sneer and a glare. A few of his brother's friends, older bikers, have a soft spot for him, but others keep their distance."

The summer he was fifteen, Ketch worked at the feedlot near town. He saved enough to buy a basket case—an old Harley-Davidson that had been taken apart years earlier. He took the motorcycle home in four large boxes. All winter he went through the parts and read about them in the oil-stained motorcycle manual. He hated the feedlot but worked there the next summer and earned enough to rebuild Black Wind.

His brother had a friend, Toby Kelzer, who owned the Sunoco.

Toby let Ketch use the garage. Finally, in September they fired up Black Wind. The old bike didn't have an electric starter, and it took about a hundred kicks to get it running. Toby looked as proud as Ketch had felt, both drenched in sweat, the engine rumbling.

"Ya know, she ain't held together by much more than spit and a prayer," Toby had said. "But I'll be damned if she ain't a fine motorcycle."

Ketch took a morning ride past Kingman and back. Hot and thirsty, he planned on getting one of the pharmacy's extra-large sodas. He pulled up in good spirits, but the high-pitched whine of an approaching engine changed that.

"Aw, man," Ketch muttered.

Darren Musgrave rode up on his red high-speed Japanese motorcycle and pulled into the next parking spot. Darren shut off his engine. "Just got back from Canyon Pass. Hell of a ride. Get a real motorcycle, Ketch, and maybe I'll let you tag along."

"I'll tell you what you can do with your crotch-rocket, Darren—"

"So, where'd you ride this morning?" Darren interrupted.

"Up to Kingman and back," Ketch mumbled.

Darren laughed. "Good idea. Keep that old junker on the straight-aways. No telling what would fall off if you leaned for a turn."

Ketch jumped off Black Wind and yanked Darren from his motorcycle by his collar. "Darren, I'm sick of you and your crap."

Darren grabbed Ketch's wrist. "Don't rip my shirt. You couldn't afford to replace it."

A shrill voice interrupted them. "Leave my brother alone, you hoodlum!"

Ketch spun and saw Darren's twelve-year-old sister, Belinda. He rolled his eyes; he liked her even less. "Darren, get her outta my face," Ketch said, releasing his shirt. "Hoodlum?"

Darren laughed. "She picked that up from Mom. Mom calls you 'that hoodlum' and 'that juvenile delinquent.'" Grinning, Darren pulled his sister into the pharmacy.

Hoodlum? Juvenile delinquent? Man, even the grown-ups have it in for me.

❊

An untouched bowl of cereal sat in front of Ketch. He had lost his appetite while reading a newspaper article about the Ripsaw Surgeon. He read one particular line again: "'The serial killer's nickname fits,' one unnamed police source revealed, 'because of his fondness for using power tools on his victims.'" Another body had been found on the outskirts of Kingman. That made nine: two in California, six in Nevada, and now one on this side of the Arizona border. The killer was making his way east one corpse at a time.

Later that day Ketch took a ride on the desert highway. He stopped in Kingman at nightfall and got gas. On his return, as he neared Canyon, he passed only one car, a sporty model of some kind that flew in the opposite direction. Though it was a long stretch of road, seeing only one car wasn't unusual; while people used the two-lane desert highway during the day, few, if any, took the road at night.

Ketch downshifted for the turn to the mesa, a longtime meeting place for Canyon teens. On any summer night you could look up and see the glow of a campfire. In the seventies the town council decided they didn't like teenagers doing who knows what up there, so they trucked a bulldozer out to push two boulders together and block the road. Everyone just parked at the boulders now and hiked the extra distance.

Ketch caught a glimpse of something off the road. Pulling a U-turn, he slowly rode up until something metallic threw back the reflection of his headlight. Ketch rolled farther into the desert sand and found Darren Musgrave's wrecked motorcycle.

"Oh, man," Ketch muttered, and killed his engine.

Darren's ride was trashed. The air smelled of gas; broken bits of red plastic littered the ground. The bike was demolished. Ketch shone the headlight around and found Darren, who was as twisted as his motorcycle.

"Darren?"

The injured boy moaned. He lay on his back, one hand balled into a fist on his stomach. The other arm lay broken and useless at his side. His legs were shattered.

Ketch knelt by the injured teen. "You jerk, you hot-dogged it one time too many."

"Help . . . Belinda," Darren moaned.

"What? Your sister was with you?"

"He . . . took her."

"Look, Darren, you have to lie still. I'll go get help."

"NO!" Darren shouted. "You have to help Belinda NOW!"

"She's not here, Darren."

"He took her," Darren repeated, opening his fist and showing Ketch another wound. Embedded into his stomach, all the way to the hilt, was a screwdriver.

"Jeez, Darren. How did you—" And then Ketch knew who had Belinda.

"He grabbed her right in front of our house. . . . I chased him."

"We can call for help. You have a cell phone, right?"

"Back home. Didn't have time to get it."

"I have to go to town for help."

"NO! He drove . . . that way." Darren pointed away from Canyon with a trembling, blood-covered hand.

The car, Ketch thought, goose bumps rising on his flesh, *the one that passed me a few minutes ago, was driven by the Ripsaw Surgeon.* If he went all the way into town for help, the killer would get away with her for sure.

"I'll go after her."

Darren didn't reply. He'd passed out.

Ketch jogged to Black Wind. Ketch knew the outcome could very well depend on how well his bike ran. He gritted his teeth as he remembered the comment Toby made when they had first started his bike. "Ain't held together by much more than spit and a prayer."

Black Wind growled as she chewed up the highway. Ketch usually didn't keep up with current events, but it was hard not to follow the Ripsaw Surgeon case. The victims' bodies were found near where they'd been taken. The car he'd seen was a small sports car, so it couldn't go into the desert. The killer would need an isolated place he could drive into.

Ketch exited at Apache Park and rode through the parking lot to the main entrance. Makes sense, Ketch thought grimly, the psycho could plug his power tools into the base of any of the streetlights here. A heavy-gauge chain hung across the entrance. A fine dusting of desert sand had blown over the road, and he didn't see any tire tracks.

"Damn. This is the only place between here and Kingman. Wait a minute—Gem City." Ketch smiled. "Yeah, Gem City."

It was a failed tourist attraction between Canyon and Kingman. In the fifties, the owners had opened a mine to pull in tourists traveling to Las Vegas. For admission visitors went into the mine with a pick and shovel and kept any gems they found. There were few, if any, gems, and Gem City closed in the late sixties. Now it was nothing more than three old buildings in the middle of nowhere.

"Gem City." The killer stopped the car a quarter-mile from the desert highway. The ramshackle buildings sat in a valley and were hidden from the road by scrub and dunes. He went to the trunk and then opened the passenger door. He smiled down at Belinda, who was bound to her reclined seat with loops of duct tape.

"Your fate awaits, my princess." The killer gestured to the old gift shop.

Belinda stared at her abductor and saw not a monster but a normal kind of guy. He was of average height, of average weight. His hair and eyes were brown. Other than being kind of geeky, nothing about the man would stand out in a crowd. When he smiled at her, however, her skin crawled. His eyes lit up with a sinister glow. The corners of his mouth stretched wide and his teeth resembled old tombstones.

Belinda lay unmoving. He squatted beside her and held up a large toolbox. "The tools of my trade." He removed a box cutter, brought her seat up from the reclined position, and cut through the tape. Belinda's hair hung raggedly. Desert dust marked the tracks her tears had taken, ending at the piece of duct tape he had slapped over her mouth. Belinda heard a loud engine on the highway and looked over the killer's shoulder.

"Don't get your hopes up, sweetie. You could yell all you wanted and they still wouldn't hear you." He sliced through the last of the tape. "Get out of the car."

⚜

Ketch parked Black Wind just off the highway behind a rocky knoll. He fished around in the leather tool bag lashed to the top of the headlight housing and removed a large wrench. Giving it a couple of test swings, he nodded and ran down the dirt road.

⚜

Holding the toolbox in one hand, the murderer pushed Belinda along with his other. At the foot of the porch steps she fell. Laughing, he nudged her with his toe until she turned and looked up at him. "Stalling won't help, sweetie. Whether I get you in there now or five minutes from now, I still have all night to play."

In a mild state of shock, she didn't initially understand the significance of the person she saw running from a clump of saguaro cactus to the madman's car.

Ketch saw two shapes in the dim light of the half-moon, and dashed from the cactus to the automobile. He was close enough to see Belinda cower on the ground. Looming over her, his back to Ketch, stood a man. *Now*, Ketch thought, and ran soft and low.

She yanked the piece of tape from her mouth and shouted. "Help! Help me!"

The Ripsaw Surgeon laughed.

Ketch swung the wrench hard and felt a great deal of satisfaction at the impact.

The madman's face went slack. He dropped his toolbox and fell to the ground. There, poised over the killer, stood Ketch in all his leather glory. Confused, Belinda stood and screamed, then she ran

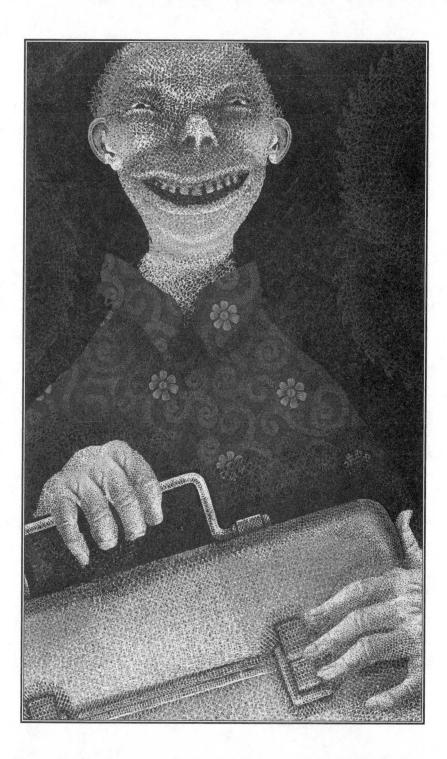

past Ketch toward the highway. *She's freaking,* he thought and gave chase. Belinda made it past the murderer's car and collapsed.

Ketch squatted by her. "Are you okay?"

She looked at him with a face covered in tears and dirt.

"How did you know—how did you—find me?"

"Your brother told me what happened. I guessed where he'd bring you."

Belinda's eyes widened. "You spoke with Darren? He's alive?"

"He's in bad shape, but yeah." Ketch helped her up. "Let's get to my bike and get out of here."

She wiped her nose on her forearm. "I'm afraid of your bike."

"Whaddya mean?"

"Darren says your bike's going to fall apart while you're riding it."

"Do you want me to leave you here?"

Belinda's lips trembled. "No—don't leave me! I'm sorry. Can't we take the crazy guy's car?"

Ketch looked at the car and then past it. They were in trouble. "Stupid, stupid, stupid," Ketch groaned. "I should have tied him up."

Belinda looked and whimpered. The killer was gone.

A small engine fired up and night turned to day. The Ripsaw Surgeon stood before stands of halogen lamps on the porch of the first building. A generator hummed at his side.

"I have two to remodel tonight instead of one. How nice. And you, the one who hit me, you will have a particularly painful death. If I were you, I'd just give up."

"Yeah, right," Ketch mumbled, tugging Belinda after him. They ran to where Ketch had hidden the Harley. He straddled it, turned a key, and fired it up with one kick.

"Get on!" he shouted.

Belinda jumped on behind him. Ketch leaned it low and gave it gas, and the back end spun, spewing dirt.

Ketch turned his head and yelled, "Street bikes aren't great on the dirt. Hold on!"

She locked her arms around his waist and shut her eyes. The tires caught heavy patches of sand, but Ketch held it upright. He turned onto the highway and cranked back the hand throttle, popping a quick wheelie.

"Watch for him. I need to concentrate!"

"You concentrate on driving! That's good!" She looked back. There was only darkness behind them. After a couple of minutes, she looked back again as headlights flared on.

"Ketch!" Belinda shouted, "It's him!"

Ketch opened the throttle. "If we can reach Canyon I can lose him on the turns and side streets!"

"He's gaining on us!" Belinda screamed.

Ketch looked in his mirror and watched the car close the distance. "We won't make it! I'll see if we can lose him at Apache Park!"

"But the park is closed at night!"

Ketch shot past the sign that announced the park's entrance

in a mile. The Ripsaw Surgeon was a car length behind them. Ketch knew if he slowed for the turn, the murderer would run them over. At the last second, Ketch swung right onto the park entrance road. The Ripsaw Surgeon's car flew past. Ketch locked the brakes, and the rear of the bike slid left. When he slowed enough, Ketch brought it back under control. The killer stopped, reversed, and turned in after them. Under a nearby streetlight, Ketch spied the chain across the entrance. Instead of slowing, Ketch increased their speed.

"What are you doing?" Belinda cried.

Ketch reached behind her left leg, patting the chrome bar attached at a vertical angle. "See these? They're crash bars. Stay in your seat, keep your legs in, and hold tight around my waist!"

Belinda looked at the motorcycle. There was another of the chrome bars behind her other leg and a larger one-piece crash bar mounted in front of the engine.

The significance of what he said hit her. "Crash bars!"

Twenty feet before the chain, Ketch leaned left and dropped the bike with a jarring *slam.* They slid along the ground. Sparks flew from the crash bars as they scraped the pavement and slipped under the chain. They came to a stop and crawled from under the motor- cycle. Ketch lifted the still-running machine and slung his leg over it. Belinda scrambled back on. Ketch accelerated into the park. Belinda turned to see the Ripsaw Surgeon park his car parallel to the chain, blocking the park entrance as a possible exit.

Apache Park was made up of three separate sections. The first, for organized sports, featured two grass-covered fields, basketball courts, and cinderblock restrooms. Past the fields to the south was the lake. North of the lake, over a small rise, was the location of the playground. Recently the safety of the old slides, swings, and merry-go-round had come into question, so the county council hired a man who designed and oversaw construction of community-built playgrounds. When completed, it would be one of those expansive wooden structures that resembled a rambling castle. While construction had not yet started, the building materials had begun to arrive. Ketch rode the bike behind a load of timber stacked past the slides and shut off the engine.

"Maybe he'll give up," Belinda suggested hopefully.

"No, that looney-toon is coming, but since he had to leave his car by the entrance, it'll take him a while to get here."

They walked through the playground to the service road entrance. It was closed off with a swinging gate that was chained to a post. Ketch pushed on the metal tubing gate, the top of which reached Belinda's chin; the bottom just cleared the ground.

"Go up the hill and look for the Ripsaw Surgeon."

"You're nuts, Ketch. Don't you watch slasher movies? Whenever someone says 'let's separate,' people start dying! No way!"

"Look, you'll be able to see him when he gets past the soccer field and have plenty of time to get back here. If you want to get out of this alive, you need to do what I say."

"Why don't you go look for him?"

"Because I'm going to figure out a way for us to get out of the park."

She glared at him.

How can a kid so young have such mean eyes? Ketch wondered. "Stay low so he can't see you." Ketch turned to a stack of lumber and started working a long, wide piece out from the metal strip that bundled the wood together.

Belinda felt like a victim in a horror movie as she trudged up the dark hill. She lay on her stomach so the Ripsaw Surgeon wouldn't see her standing against the light of the half-moon sky.

She thought back to when she'd been snatched. Her parents were out for the evening, and Darren had been in the garage applying yet another coat of wax to his motorcycle. Belinda went to get the mail from the street-side mailbox.

"Don't forget to take out the garbage, Darren," she told him.

"Don't have to now that you're taking yourself to the curb," he'd answered.

"Ha, ha. Very funny."

The Ripsaw Surgeon took her as she was thumbing through the mail. He threw her over his shoulder, and the mail scattered like leaves. At first she thought it was Darren and tried to wriggle off his shoulder. The man punched her in the side. She looked back at her house and saw Darren at his bike. She tried to yell, but the punch had robbed her of air. The killer threw her in his car, and Darren glanced up as they drove off.

Belinda had pressed herself against the passenger door of the small sports car and reached for the handle, but the man had sawed it off. A few blocks later she heard the high-pitched whine of Darren's motorcycle. The man looked in the rearview mirror and grinned. Speeding, her kidnapper drove out of town, with Darren close behind them. At the mesa road, the man slammed his foot on the brake. There was a horrendous thump, and the car rocked. The man pulled a U-turn and crept forward until the headlights illuminated Darren's wrecked bike. Just past it, Darren struggled to sit up.

"Stay here," the killer growled. He reached under his seat and took out a long screwdriver. He walked to Darren and pushed him back down. The madman knelt beside her brother and lifted the screwdriver high over his head.

Belinda shut her eyes and screamed.

He returned to the car and bound her with duct tape.

⟨◈⟩

Distant movement caught Belinda's attention. He was coming. Belinda crawled back from the top of the hill, stood, and ran to Ketch.

"He's close," she panted. "He'll be here in a minute."

"Good," Ketch said, and led her behind the lumber.

"Good? Did you say good?"

"Shut up." Ketch leaned past the lumber, watching.

"What's the plan?" Belinda whispered.

Ketch smiled and mounted his bike. "Get on. I fixed it so we can get out by the service road."

"Why did we wait for him to get so close?"

"So he'll have farther to get back to his car. We'll have more time to get to town."

Ketch jumped on the kickstarter and the motorcycle blasted to life. He swung wide around the lumber pile and saw the killer, toolbox in hand, jogging down the hill toward them. Ketch straightened the bike and headed toward the service road exit.

Belinda peeked over his shoulder. "You have got to be kidding!"

"Just hang on!" he yelled back.

Ketch hadn't opened the gates. Instead, a long wooden plank leaned against it. They hit the makeshift ramp and were airborne. The rear of the motorcycle dropped low and keeled to the left. Belinda, sure they would crash, screamed. With a bone-jarring thump, they were down—down and upright—and heading for the highway.

"Don't—you—ever," Belinda screamed at Ketch, accentuating each word with a punch to his back, "do—that—again!"

Ketch swung the bike onto the highway and accelerated toward home. He looked back at Belinda and smiled. She smiled in return. The bike shuddered, and Ketch's grin faltered. The motorcycle decelerated while emitting rapid pops.

"Not now!" Ketch yelled.

"What now?" Belinda shrieked.

Ketch braked to the side of the road and shut off the motor. "Fouled a plug. It'll take a few minutes."

"We don't have a few minutes!"

He knelt by the left side of the bike and yanked the adjustable wrench from his pocket. He detached the plug cables and unscrewed the front sparkplug. Using a dirty red bandanna as a hot pad, he held the plug in the beam of his headlight.

"Bingo." Ketch pulled a new plug from the leather tool bag and screwed it in. "Hang on to this." Ketch handed her the fouled plug wrapped in the bandanna.

They were nearly to Canyon when the killer caught up with them. Ketch had the throttle opened flat out. They neared the spot where he had found Darren. In a passing flash, Ketch saw a bit of broken chrome reflect his high beam. They passed the city limits sign and flew by side streets. The killer sped too close for Ketch to slow and make a turn.

"That plug I gave you—throw it over your shoulder!"

Belinda removed it from the bandanna and threw it hard and level behind her. The sparkplug bounced from the psycho's windshield, but made enough impact so that he slowed. Ketch braked and turned onto Sequoia Road. The Ripsaw Surgeon followed. In the glow of a streetlight, Belinda saw webbed cracks running through his windshield. The high-speed game of tag continued through town. Ketch made one turn after another, keeping the Ripsaw Surgeon from getting too close. They gained an even bigger lead at Hudson Road. Mrs. Appleton, the town's oldest person, pulled into the intersection in her 1966 Cadillac. When she saw the motorcycle and car racing toward her, she panicked and stopped. There was just enough room for Black Wind to squeeze behind her, but the killer had to skid to a stop and wait for Mrs. Appleton to get out of the way.

"How come there's never a cop when you want one?" Ketch yelled over his shoulder.

"Go by the police station and honk your horn!" Belinda shouted.

"Worth a try!" Ketch swung onto Jefferson Street hoping that Herschel, the lone cop who worked nights, would be there. Ketch shook his head; one lousy policeman on night duty. Just another reason to hate this crummy little town.

When they got within a block of the police station Ketch pressed his thumb onto the horn button, letting loose a weak, frog croak blast. He didn't let up on the horn until well past the station. *Probably didn't even hear the horn over my loud pipes,* Ketch thought. *But if Herschel hears me racing down Jefferson, he'll be hot to nail me.*

"I didn't see any lights on at the station!" Belinda yelled.

Ketch glanced into the rearview mirror and saw the Ripsaw Surgeon was closing the distance. Ketch scraped the crash bars leaning into a right turn, then made three lefts, going around the block. There was no activity when they went back by the police station.

"Damn! Herschel must be out on patrol!"

Black Wind shuddered and chugged. Ketch reached down and fiddled with something under the gas tank, making the bike run fine again. "That was the gas. We're on reserve. We're gonna run out soon, and that creep will roll right over us!"

Belinda wanted to cry. What a horrible night. She'd been kidnapped. Her rescuer turned out to be Ketch. They'd ridden at deadly speeds. They'd skidded under the chain and flown over the gate, and still that wacko was on their tail. What death-defying stunt would it take to get away?

She had a thought. It was crazy. She replayed it in her mind and a smile broke on her face. "I have an idea!" As they weaved through the streets of Canyon, she shouted her plan to Ketch. "Too dangerous?" she asked when she finished.

"Definitely," he shouted back. "That's why I like it!"

They crossed over to Helms Boulevard, turned right at Brighton's Hardware, right onto Grimsley, past Canyon High, left on Sequoia, and back onto the desert highway.

Ketch turned onto the mesa road. "This is it!"

The Ripsaw Surgeon took advantage of the dirt road and accelerated, while Ketch barely maintained control. The killer drove less than a foot behind.

"Go for it!" Belinda yelled.

Ketch's headlight danced off the twin boulders blocking the road. The gap between the two was impossibly narrow, yet Ketch increased their speed. The boulders loomed ahead, and Belinda braced for the inevitable impact. Instead, they shot through the two monoliths like a bullet through a gun barrel.

The ground shook as the Ripsaw Surgeon's car hit the rocks. The *whoomph* of impact drowned out the motorcycle engine. It wasn't like the movies; the car did not explode, but crumpled into an unrecognizable mass of metal.

Ketch shut off his bike, and they stood on shaky legs.

"Come on," Ketch said. "Let's get some help for your brother."

He pulled her tightly to his side so that she wouldn't look into the twisted wreckage as they walked past.

Chris rolled up the pages of his story and shoved them in his pocket.

Kara sat at the edge of the sofa and cleared her throat. "I find it interesting how much Chris has in common with Chelsea."

Chris laughed, and Chelsea snorted.

"Seriously," Kara said. "The motorcycle symbolizes Chelsea's desire for freedom from Maplewood, but it also symbolizes the freedom Chris strives for from his father."

"That's a bunch of psychobabble crap," Chris muttered.

Ian Tremblin applauded. "An excellent story, and your own creation gives you something to ponder. Please lower the candle count, Chris."

Chris stepped to the candelabrum.

"Let that be another lesson for you budding writers," Ian Tremblin said. "The only protagonist more exciting than a hero is a reluctant hero."

Chris blew out a candle.

"That brings our candle count to four."

"How are we doing, Mr. Tremblin? Any favorites yet?" Demarius asked.

"Not yet, but one of you, because of tonight, will become a published author."

"That would be great," Chelsea said. "Can you imagine seeing your very own book at a bookstore? I can't tell you how many of those how-to-be-a-writer books I've read. I guess they work, 'cause here I am."

Demarius's eyes glowed. "I want to be the first African American known for horror. Black authors have tackled horror, but none are known as horror authors. Not in the way you look at Stephen King or Mr. Tremblin. What about you, Wade?"

I shrugged. "I like writing, I guess. I do it for fun. I never really thought about being a professional writer. To be honest, I don't really care if I win. Being here and making it through the entire night will be good enough for me."

"For me it goes back to my dad," Chris said. "He'd kill me if he knew I wrote or painted or that I was here tonight. Writing and painting, to him, are distractions from football. But if I actually got published, what could he say? Maybe then I could get out of sports and into stuff I really like."

"Though only one of you will win," the author said, "you are all gifted writers."

"Thanks." Chelsea beamed.

"Don't be too accepting, Chelsea. Look at the fate of many famous writers—Ernest Hemingway, John Kennedy Toole, Hunter S. Thompson, and Robert E. Howard. Study their lives, and you'll see the gift of writing can also be a curse."

The writer looked around the room. "Have you noticed how the encircling darkness closes in with each extinguished wick?" The room was a gloomy chamber. The flickering candles caused shadows to come to life, dancing and jumping around us.

"I like the darkness. It's romantic. Don't you think, Chelsea?" Chris winked.

"You had your chance," Chelsea said.

"Why do I feel there is a history between you two?" Ian Tremblin asked.

Chelsea sniffed and looked away.

" 'Cause there's a history between us," Chris said.

"Shut up, Chris. It's nobody's business."

Chris shrugged and sat. "Fine. If you want it to be a secret, it'll remain a secret."

Ian Tremblin shrugged. "Very well. I guess we will move along to—"

Chris shot forward. "Okay, if you insist. I broke Chelsea's heart."

"You lie!" she shouted.

"Yep, it was a terrible thing. Clearly she's never gotten over it."

"Oh, puh-lease."

Chris jumped to his feet. "It was the summer before last. My family took a trip to Florida. Guess who I met on those white sandy beaches? A lovely, lonely, impressionable redhead named Chelsea Flynt."

Chelsea stepped up to Chris. "You are so full of it."

"She was all tan, with the cutest freckles on her face and shoulders." He leaned toward Demarius and me. "And let me tell ya, she's hot in a bikini."

"Creep!"

"She was amazed when this handsome young athlete walked into her life."

"Yeah, I met him on the beach, and yeah, we got along. But he only told me lies. He said he was an artist. A painter, he said—and a writer."

"Surprise, Chelsea, I'm here tonight. I can write, but get to the romance."

"The romance? Sloppy kisses is more like it. Oh, and we actually started planning a future. He'd major in the arts and write and illustrate books. We'd go to the same college, he said.

You heard him, no way he'd major in the arts. *Daddy* won't let you, will he?"

Chris sat, amusement gone from his face. "Look, Chelsea, I was on vacation. No one knew me. I could be who I wanted to be, or at least pretend. How was I supposed to know you'd be moving here?"

"I couldn't believe it when Dad got transferred to Maplewood. The fact that I'd be reunited with Chris made the move seem preordained or something. We'd been e-mailing, so I shared the news. I began to hear from him less and less until the e-mails from Mr. Sensitive-Artsy-Type stopped altogether."

"Come on, Chelsea. At first I was glad you were coming, then I realized there'd be no hiding the fact that I'm not exactly who you thought I was."

"No, *not exactly* who I thought you were."

"Excuse me," Ian Tremblin interrupted. "A question from the peanut gallery, if you don't mind."

"Huh?" Chris said.

"Yeah, sure, I guess," Chelsea said.

"If he had told you that he was actually a regionally famous football star instead of a Thoreau-slash-Rembrandt hopeful, would you have still been interested in him?"

"Of course."

"Yeah, right," Chris said. "Do you remember that first day, a couple of hours after I met you? We'd been riding Boogie Boards and got out of the surf to sit on the beach."

"I remember."

"Do you remember a group of guys just down the beach throwing a football?"

"No."

"So you don't remember what you said?"

"What are you getting at, Chris?"

"One of them missed the ball, and it landed by us. It kicked up a little sand on us—only a little. The guy ran over, said 'sorry,' and picked up the ball. When he ran back, you shook your head and said 'stupid jocks.'"

"I did not."

"You did. After that, I wasn't going to tell you I played football."

Chelsea paced. "It doesn't excuse what happened at the mall."

Chris sighed. "No, it doesn't."

Chelsea sat, her feet in the chair. She crossed her arms over her knees, resting her chin there.

"I detest unfinished stories," Ian Tremblin finally said.

Chris rubbed a hand over his head. "You tell it, Chelsea."

She looked at him. "Well, I moved to Maplewood at the beginning of last summer. I e-mailed Chris to let him know, but he didn't reply, of course. Six or seven months later, I went to a movie with some friends. Actually, we went to see *Curse of the Wampyr*, Mr. Tremblin."

"Oh, what a hatchet job they did with my story. I was ashamed to have my name associated with that film."

"We liked it. Anyway, we were in the mall parking lot looking for my friend's car, and a van pulled up. The side door slid open, and someone yelled, 'Here's a little color for your wardrobe.' I heard popping sounds and felt these painful little stings on my body. They were shooting us with paintball guns. Colorful spatters were exploding all over us—red, yellow, green. I yelled 'stop it!' One of the guys in the van told the others to quit."

"It was me," Chris said. "We'd been partyin'. One of the guys wanted to go mess with some geeks. Another guy goes out to the paintball range all the time and has a bunch of equipment. One thing led to another. We went cruisin' the mall and saw these goths, these vampire wannabes. I didn't recognize Chelsea at first. Her hair was black, she was all pale. But when she yelled, I knew her voice."

Chelsea smiled sadly. "I said, 'Chris, is that you?' He turned away and told the driver to leave."

"My, my. That certainly is a tale of teen angst," Ian Tremblin said.

"Yeah, well"—Chris drained his final bottle of water—"confession may be good for the soul, but all this water has filled my bladder. I'll go brave the bathroom." He nodded toward the dim outline of the bedroom suite doorway.

"Put a candle in the lantern and take it with you," Ian Tremblin suggested.

"Nah, I'll be fine." Chris departed the dwindling circle of light.

"I suppose it's my turn, huh?" I asked.

"Yes, but let's wait for Chris to return." Ian Tremblin sat by the candelabrum and stroked his long beard.

Chris called from the other room, "Don't wait for me. Gotta let my eyes adjust before I—uh—get down to business. I can hear fine from—" A crash resonated from the bedroom suite and startled us. "Oops. Sorry 'bout that. Knocked a picture off the wall. Hey! Just found the bed in here. Aaahh, comfortable— musty, though."

Ian Tremblin shrugged. "Go ahead then, Wade."

"Excuse me. I've wanted to leave for a long time," Kara said, "but I never go."

"Yes, your departure has been a long time coming, hasn't it?" Tremblin said. "But now we're at another impasse."

Kara looked resigned. "How so?"

"You've sat through everyone else's tales. Everyone but Wade, the young man who has generously comforted you on more than one occasion tonight. Of all the finalists, you should at least hear his story."

"That's all right, Kara. It won't hurt my feelings if you want to get out of here."

Kara hugged herself. "No, Mr. Tremblin is right."

"Ready, Mr. Reilly?" Tremblin asked.

"In a moment." I went to my bedroll and unrolled it, taking out a handful of pages. I stood before the dim glow of the candles, cleared my throat, and began.

A Countdown to Infestation

SEVEN HUNDRED TWO HOURS TO GO

"No problem, Mr. Columbo. I can do your yard today."

"Wonderful, Justin." The man threw an arm over Justin's shoulders. Mr. Columbo had never been this touchy-feely. He seemed strange since returning from his Florida vacation.

"Uh, what's up? Why the big yard job?" Justin had stopped by to give the yard its weekly mowing, and Mr. Columbo had asked if Justin could do some additional landscaping chores.

Mr. Columbo was sixtyish with thin gray hair. He dressed nondescriptly in black slacks, a white button-down shirt, and brown loafers. His house was set apart from the rest of the homes, surrounded on three sides by woods.

"What's up," Mr. Columbo leaned in and whispered to Justin, "is my wife arrives this afternoon!"

"Your what?"

"My wife, Justin, my boy. Yep, I finally gave up the life of confirmed bachelorhood. Wait until you meet Leta. She is a beautiful woman."

"You're married?"

"Our little secret? Mum's the word, okay? I met her on my vacation. Crazy, huh?"

"Well . . . not if you believe in love at first sight, I guess," Justin said.

"That's exactly what it was. See, I took a side trip from Orlando and ended up in a quaint village called Cassadaga. I saw the strangest thing in that town. Police cars and all these black sedans and vans were parked in front of a small Victorian house. Men in suits and sunglasses stood around talking into cell phones. I looked at them and thought FBI or CIA. Three men, covered head to foot in shiny material, got out of a van. They had big tanks strapped to their backs and carried these—well, they looked like flamethrowers. What is this, I thought, a terrorist raid? A policeman motioned traffic to keep moving, so I didn't see what happened. I stopped at a little restaurant to get a bite and find out what was going on. I walked in, and there she sat, my lovely Leta. You know I'm a shy man, but when I saw this beautiful woman sitting at a table and sobbing—yes, she was crying—I offered my assistance."

"Why was she crying?"

"A terrible thing," Mr. Columbo said. "She'd just lost her family to a house fire. She wouldn't go into detail, said she didn't want to dwell on it. We spent hours together. I've never felt that close, that comfortable with a woman. She was leaving town, though she didn't know where she would go. I talked her into going to Orlando with me. She got a room at my hotel, and I spent the rest of my vacation with her. The poor woman was so distraught, and I did my best to comfort her. One night we drove to Daytona. After dinner, as we walked along the beach, she took my hand. I told her I would do anything for her, anything to help her get over her loss. She stopped there at the water's edge, took my face in her hands, and kissed me.

"'Oh, Leta,' I told her, 'if you hadn't had such a terrible thing just happen, I would ask for your hand in marriage right on the spot.' And you know what she did, Justin? She said yes, just like it had been a real proposal instead of me talking about one. She said she believed things happened for a purpose, and she believed it was fate that made me walk through the door of that restaurant that day. I wanted to wait until her mourning had passed, but Leta insisted it was the right thing to do and wanted to marry immediately. So, we found a beautiful small church the next day, and our knot, as they say, was tied."

"Wow! I didn't know you had it in you, Mr. Columbo!"

"I know, I know. It isn't like me to do something so sponta-neous. Anyway, she had some affairs to attend to. I have to attend to some things myself before I get her at the airport. I'll be gone when you're done. Can I pay you tomorrow?"

"Sure. So what was going down at that house you passed?"

Mr. Columbo pursed his lips. "I got so swept away meeting Leta that I forgot to ask anyone."

⊰◊⊱

SIX HUNDRED EIGHTY-ONE HOURS TO GO

Justin parked his bike behind Mr. Columbo's old Buick and noticed how close Mr. Columbo had come to denting it on the huge cement planter. He walked under the carport, pulled open the side screen door, and knocked.

"What do you want?"

A woman stood in the backyard beside the storage shed. Justin was struck dumb by her beauty. Was she Mr. Columbo's new wife? Wow! She had to be twenty years younger than him, at least. Tall and lean, she had lustrous raven black hair. Black eyes glowed from her dark-complexioned face. She wore tight black slacks and a black blouse. Even though the day was warm, black gloves covered her hands.

"I said what do you want?"

"Um, hi. Uh, is Mr. Columbo here?"

"Who are you?"

"I'm Justin. Mr. Columbo owes me for some yard work. Are you Mrs. Columbo?"

The woman stared at Justin. A smile came to her lips. "I'm sorry for being rude, Justin. Yes, I'm Mrs. Columbo." She stepped closer. "He told you we were married?"

"Yes, ma'am."

"That naughty man. We were going to keep it a secret until after I arrived."

"Can I talk to Mr. Columbo?"

"I'm afraid he's still in bed, dear."

"It's almost noon."

"Well," Mrs. Columbo purred, "we are newlyweds, after all. I kept him up late."

"Oh."

"You're blushing. How delicious. Now tell me, how much do we owe you?"

A few minutes later, as he rode away, Justin couldn't shake the feeling that something was not right.

<hr>

FIVE HUNDRED NINETEEN HOURS TO GO

Justin parked his bike by the driveway and noticed that either Mr. Columbo hadn't moved his car all week or he had parked dangerously close to the planter again. He wrinkled his nose as he strode toward the storage shed that held the lawn mower.

"Whew! Something's rotten in the trashcans," he muttered, and broke through a spiderweb as he walked by the big oak between the carport and shed. "Ugh!" He brushed wildly at his face. "I hate spiders." He looked around and noticed more webs. Large ones entangled the bushes that ran the length of the house. He couldn't even begin to count the number of webs under the eaves. Justin opened the shed and grabbed a can of insecticide from the shelf by the door. Where to begin? He took the can to the corner of the house, aimed under the eaves, and sprayed. Several spiders, fleeing the poison, spun down. Justin sprayed again and they died, hanging from their threads like eight-legged yo-yos.

Taking a step, Justin kicked something. An object wrapped in white material stuck out from under a bush by the back patio. It was pretty big, about the size of a dog, he thought. The ripe odor seemed more intense. Curiosity got the best of him, and he dragged it out.

"What are you doing?"

Startled, Justin jumped up and found himself face-to-face with Mrs. Columbo.

"What is that?" she screamed, and pointed at the can of insecticide.

"Well, there are all these spiderwebs back here and—" He held up the can.

"Don't point that at me!"

"I'm not pointing it, I'm just—I mean—um, well. Is Mr. Columbo here?"

The woman leered at Justin, a snarl on her lips. "Throw that poison into the trash."

Unable to speak, Justin shook the can to demonstrate that it was half full. Her eyes narrowed, and she pointed a gloved finger toward the trashcans. He walked into the carport with Mrs. Columbo on his heels and threw the can away.

"I thought you handled the lawn. I didn't know you were in charge of pest control as well." Her voice dripped sarcasm.

"I came to cut the lawn. This is the day I do it. I saw the webs and . . ."

She looked at the shed and saw the open door. "Did you go inside?"

"No."

"No?"

"I mean, yes."

"Yes?"

"I mean, I opened the door to get the bug spray, but I didn't actually go in."

Mrs. Columbo put her hands on her hips and looked at the backyard. "I don't think we need your services this week, Justin."

"Is Mr. Columbo here?"

She leaned forward until their faces almost touched. "Mr. Columbo is sick and can't get out of bed." The smell of rancid garbage was not as thick where they stood, yet when Mrs. Columbo spoke, he recognized the same fetid odor on her breath.

THREE HUNDRED FIFTY-ONE HOURS TO GO

Justin wasn't eager to go to the Columbos' house. He decided he'd quit if Mrs. Columbo gave him any grief.

On the way, Marjorie Sawyer, a neighbor and a friend, called out to him. "Hey, Justin, have you seen Champ anywhere?" Champ was the Sawyers' playful German shepherd, or as Marjorie called him, her snuggle shepherd.

"No, sorry, Marjorie. I'll keep an eye out for him."

"Mom let him out last night, and he never came back."

"He probably found a girlfriend."

"So many pets have disappeared over the past week. I'm way worried."

"Really? Other animals are missing?" Justin got off his bike.

"I swear, Justin, if something isn't right in front of your face you don't see it." She dragged him to the streetlight at the corner. A number of multicolored flyers were nailed to the wooden pole. Each had a picture of a dog or a cat and the word MISSING.

"If you see Champ, bring him home, okay?"

"I will. I hope you find him."

Mr. Columbo's car sat in the same exact spot. A putrid stench greeted him as he walked to the shed, and a surge of nausea brought on a moment of dizziness.

He gagged. "Oh, man, it's worse. I'm gonna be sick right here."

Tracking down the source wasn't difficult. It was thicker by the garbage cans. He lifted a lid and was greeted by a blast of foul air. Holding his breath, he looked in and saw several objects covered in the same material he'd discovered under the bush the previous week. Justin poked at one a couple of times. The material itself had some elasticity, and the object it covered was spongy, so he could push it in a little bit with his finger. Maybe that was how Mrs. Columbo bagged her trash.

"Yeah, that's it." Mr. Columbo is still sick, he rationalized, too sick to take the trash to the curb. Mrs. Columbo, on the other hand, doesn't know what day the garbage truck comes, so the trash sits and gets stinkier.

He set off for the shed but stopped briefly when he saw more spiderwebs in the back. Why hadn't she let him kill the spiders? He noticed something else: There were more of those wrapped things stuffed under the bushes. The smell was just as bad back there. At the shed he saw a padlock. He stared a moment. Why was the shed locked?

He knocked at the side door, and Mrs. Columbo opened it immediately. "I, uh, I need the key to get into the shed so I can get the lawn mower."

She said nothing.

"How is Mr. Columbo? Is he feeling any better?"

"You may speak with him, if you wish. But you'll have to come inside." He looked past her. Every curtain had been drawn.

The door opened to a dark lair. "Come, come," she said, beckoning with one long, gloved finger.

A strange sound, a loud *whoosh*, interrupted my narration.

"Did you hear—?"

The noise continued as we looked to Ian Tremblin. He shrugged.

"Whoa, man! That's some heavy-duty plumbing."

"Chris!" Chelsea and I said together.

"Hey, guys!" Chris called from the other room. "They had some powerful toilets in the old days. Did you hear that? Thought it was gonna suck me down."

Everyone laughed except Chelsea. "Quit fooling around and get back in here."

"In a minute. Mom always says to practice good hygiene. Gotta wash my hands."

"He's going to take forever," Chelsea said. "Go on with your story, Wade."

"Just a minute, I lost my place. Wait, here it is—"

"Come, come," she said, beckoning with one long, gloved finger.

He took a step, then stopped. "No, thank you, Mrs. Columbo. I don't want to disturb your husband. If you'll get the key to the shed, I'll mow the lawn."

Mrs. Columbo looked into the street, then at him. Staring, she leaned closer. The moment stretched, and Justin felt as if he were in a suspenseful movie at a key scene. She almost touched him. Then Marjorie whizzed by on her bike and waved.

Mrs. Columbo stepped back into the house. "We no longer need your services," she said, and slammed the door.

Even though he'd just been fired, Justin left the Columbos' with a sense of relief. He felt he'd escaped with something far more precious than a job.

⌘

ONE HUNDRED SEVENTEEN HOURS TO GO

Justin aimlessly rode his bike. His thoughts focused on the Columbos, particularly the wife. For some reason, he felt there was a connection between her and the missing pets, but for the life of him, he couldn't figure out what that connection was.

An unctuous odor brought Justin back from his reverie to discover he'd unintentionally ridden to the Columbo house. He coasted to a stop by the curb and made a face; the rotten smell had now reached the street. The spiderwebs were no longer confined to the back but strung around the front. As he watched, the shed door opened, and Mrs. Columbo exited. Oblivious to him, she walked under the carport. She carried something round and white and larger than a basketball. There were nodules on the surface. Strings of white fabric dragged the ground. She held the ball to her cheek and caressed it. Her lips moved as if she were talking to it.

"You'd think she was holding a baby," Justin mumbled.

She carried it into the house. A moment later she emerged, went to the shed, and retrieved another one. When she got a third, she glanced up and saw him. Clutching the sphere to her chest, she stood and stared until Justin forced himself to pedal away.

⚜

SIXTY-EIGHT HOURS TO GO

Justin woke with a start. The answer had come as he slept. It would tie together Mrs. Columbo's strange behavior, why he hadn't seen Mr. Columbo, the missing animals, the white balls, and the horrendous odor. Justin dressed quickly and ran out of the house into the morning sunshine. A quick bike ride brought him to his destination. He hid his bike in some brush down the road from the Columbo home. He ducked into the woods across the street and made his way in the general direction of the house. Even at a distance, he could smell the odor. It no longer reminded him of garbage. Now he associated the smell with death. Justin didn't hurry; instead he trod slowly through the woods, looking for spiders, webs, or fabric-wrapped objects. He picked his way through the brush until he got close enough to see the house.

The once-pristine home looked run-down. Overgrown grass and weeds choked the formerly perfect lawn. Each corner, nook, and cranny provided shelter to spiders that generously spun their webs, giving the house a gossamer quality.

Two hours later he still sat behind a tree, waiting. A door slammed, startling him. He pushed apart some low-hanging limbs and saw the woman in black. He leaned forward as she stepped into the street and saw her carrying cans of cat food and a box of dog biscuits.

"Baiting your traps, Mrs. Columbo?" he said to himself.

She walked down half a block and disappeared into the woods. Justin darted from cover and ran across the street and up the driveway. He opened the side screen and tried the door; it was unlocked. He opened it and peered into Mr. Columbo's den. Everything was there: the furniture, large-screen TV, and wood paneling. New to the room, however, was webbing. The den was coated in spun material. A particularly dense and tangled web hung from the ceiling in the far corner. Suspended in it, like planets in the cosmos, were three white orbs.

"Egg sacs," he muttered, feeling small hairs rise on the back of his neck.

Justin heard footsteps. He silently closed the door and slipped around to the back of the house. He stepped into a large mass of spiderwebs and fought the urge to run. Peering around the corner, he saw Mrs. Columbo walk up the driveway. She carried another fabric-wrapped, or web-spun, object. Slightly larger than a loaf of bread, it mewed and wriggled. Mrs. Columbo disappeared into the house with her living parcel.

Justin ran under the carport toward the street. He stole a quick glance through the window and stopped. Mrs. Columbo stood with her back to him. She lifted the squirming package to her mouth. Justin dropped below the window and sat hard. His breath came shallow and fast. He wanted to run, but the sight left him dizzy. Instead, he worked at calming himself. Only then did he lift his head and peer into the shadowy room again. He watched, unbelieving, as Mrs. Columbo lifted her body into the tangled nest that housed the egg sacs, finally coming to rest, her body gently swaying upside down in the web.

⟨◇⟩

THIRTY-SEVEN HOURS TO GO

The black widow species Latrodectus hesperus *is common in the western states while* L. mactans *is found in the central and eastern regions of the U.S.*

Justin scrolled through the Web site he'd found on black widow spiders. He'd decided on that species after comparing one of the site's photographs of egg sacs with what he had seen at Mr. Columbo's house.

Black widow venom is fifteen times as toxic as that of rattlesnakes. The female is usually found hanging belly up in the web. Perhaps the most infamous trait of the spider is how the female consumes the male after mating.

"Poor Mr. Columbo," Justin said.

During a reproductive session the female will produce between one and nine egg sacs. Each egg sac contains 250 to 900 eggs.

"Nine hundred eggs! I saw three egg sacs. That's over two thousand babies!"

The incubation period for black widow eggs is up to thirty days.

"Time's almost up." Justin decided to go to the police. But first he'd have to get evidence. "Photographs."

⚜

TWO HOURS TO GO

Justin filled a backpack with what he'd need, including a small digital camera. He dressed in a long-sleeved black T-shirt, black sweatpants, black socks, and sneakers. He sat quietly until he was sure his parents were asleep.

⚜

FORTY-FIVE MINUTES TO GO

The night had a tomblike quiet. The only sound came from his bicycle wheels singing on the pavement. Instead of stopping at his destination, he raced past on a reconnaissance run. The house sat dark. Justin decided he'd leave his bike at the end of Mr. Columbo's driveway for a quick getaway.

⚜

THIRTY MINUTES TO GO

Justin took photos of the web-shrouded house. He also photographed the web-spun carcasses stuffed under the bushes. He felt somewhat safe using the flash, because the den, where Mrs. Columbo nested, had no window facing the backyard. He wheeled one of the trashcans around back and opened the lid. The concentrated, greasy odor of death was too much and Justin tied a bandanna around his face. Disgusted at what he had to do, Justin reached to the top object and tore the spun webbing from it. It was like pulling at thick cotton. After a muted ripping, Justin found himself staring into the dead eyes of Champ, the missing German shepherd. Biting back a cry, he looked at the lifeless animal. Champ's face, front legs, and shoulders were visible in the moonlight. Clumps of hair had fallen out, and the hair that remained stuck out like bristles. Flesh sunk against bones. Justin remembered reading on the Web site: *Black widows eat by sucking bodily fluids out of their victims.* He swallowed hard, stepped back, and took a couple of photographs, hoping Marjorie would never see them.

❀

TEN MINUTES TO GO

Justin circled the house. He stopped at two windows that opened onto Mr. Columbo's bedroom. Both were locked and the blinds drawn. While a photo of a web-wrapped Mr. Columbo would help convince the police, he was relieved he wouldn't be able to get one. He didn't want to remember his kind neighbor as dead and sucked dry.

FIVE MINUTES TO GO

Justin peeked into the den. Looking into the dark house at night was like trying to look through a blackboard. He considered holding the camera to the window and aiming in the direction of the nest but knew he'd only get a photo of the flash reflected in the glass. There was only one way to get a picture of Mrs. Columbo in her web. Justin tightened the straps on his backpack and tiptoed to the door. He pulled open the screen, thankful that Mr. Columbo kept the hinges well oiled, and then slowly opened the door. He put the camera to his eye, aimed it, and pressed the button. The flash lit the room for a brief second, long enough for Justin to see that Mrs. Columbo was not in the web.

"My goodness, you've come at such a late hour." Mrs. Columbo stood at the front of the carport. Because of the bright moon behind her, Justin could only see her silhouette.

In his mind Justin was already running, but sheer terror kept him from moving.

"You know what I think? No one knows you're here. I think you snuck out to come take photos, you naughty boy. They wouldn't believe you without them. In fact, if you were to disappear, no one would think to look here. And, Justin—I'm so hungry."

Mrs. Columbo shook. Her body tensed, and she made a straining growl as she ripped away her clothes. Her silhouette changed. Instead of two arms and two legs, four more appendages were visible. Half turning into the moonlight, she allowed Justin a momentary glimpse of a crimson hourglass on her naked belly. That gave Justin the inspiration to run. He dashed to the backyard. Behind him, Mrs. Columbo laughed. He turned at the corner and ran to the woods abutting the yard. He leapt over a small bush and found himself frozen in place. He tried to run, but his body wouldn't respond. Each time he attempted to pull away, he found himself caught more tightly.

"Nooo!" He had run into a giant web. He looked back as Mrs. Columbo stepped into the backyard. Dropping forward, she scuttled toward him on all eight limbs. Justin panicked and fought against the web. Both legs and his left arm were immobile. Reaching over his right shoulder with his one free arm, Justin managed to grab the zipper on his backpack. He opened it as far as his limited reach would allow. What he reached for had been the last thing he had put in, therefore it was at the top. He grunted in pain as he stretched, fearing he would wrench his shoulder out of its socket. His fingers finally found it, and he lifted the can of insecticide from the backpack. Mrs. Columbo was right behind him, and her two front legs reached for him.

He struggled to flip the lid off. "Stupid safety cap." Trying a different tack, he leaned back and found he had enough room to maneuver the can between his thighs. Mrs. Columbo's spider limbs touched him, stroking his head and neck. Bracing for the bite of the black widow, he wrenched the cap from the can, twisted in the web, and shot a blast of insecticide directly into Mrs. Columbo's face. Her mouth stretched wide, but instead of a scream, she produced a phlegmy clicking. Spider legs wiped madly at her face as she backed away. She glared at Justin through bloodshot eyes and charged. He waited until she was almost on him and sprayed, dousing her head. She backed away and came again, but her legs buckled and she fell at Justin's feet. She rolled onto her back. Her eight limbs twitched and curled over her crimson belly.

⚜

SECONDS TO GO

Justin tossed the empty can. "Kills on contact? Not hardly!"

After some experimentation he found he could free himself if he worked on one strand at a time. It would take a while, maybe hours, but at least he wouldn't have to worry about being dinner. Justin worked his left arm free and had started on his right leg when a slamming screen door broke his concentration. The door slammed again, and then again. He twisted around until he saw a small child under the carport.

"Hey! Hey, you, kid! I need some help. Go call the police, please."

The child—he couldn't tell if it was a boy or girl—stood and watched.

"Come on, I need help!"

Another figure joined the first, and then another, until there was a group. Justin froze, cold fingers of fear running up his spine. He knew who they were. The small children dropped to their bellies and skittered his way, hungry after freeing themselves from egg sacs. Justin watched as they came closer, wishing that he'd brought more than one can of bug spray.

INFESTATION

"You are truly disturbed," Chelsea said, pissing me off.

I snapped at her, "What do you mean, I'm disturbed?"

"I mean your story is—well—it's disturbing."

She didn't mean anything by it. No way she could know the doubts I had about my sanity. I shook my head and rubbed my face. "Sorry. Didn't mean to snap at you. I guess I'm a little stressed."

"I believe you need to lower our candle count, Wade," Ian Tremblin said.

"Yeah, sure." I pinched a wick between my index finger and thumb. Three candles, a third of the original number, didn't produce enough light for the room. We instinctively scooted our chairs closer. The candlelight mirrored in Ian Tremblin's eyes looked like flickering stars.

"Wade, you pretty much described what hell would be like for me," Chelsea said. "Giant spiders." She shook her entire body like she was trying to dislodge any bugs that might be on her. "Actually, to make it totally unbearable you'd have to throw in giant snakes, too."

"It's a powerful story indeed that can make someone ponder the torments of hell, Wade. Congratulations," Tremblin said. "And it will carry on to the rest of us. Chelsea's reaction to your story has planted a seed that may very well germinate one sleepless night as we lie in bed. We'll remember the story and how it invokes Chelsea's personal hell, then we'll wonder what eternal damnation would be for us. Maybe the creepy-crawlies that Chelsea fears? Hell, for a claustrophobic, could be eternal confinement in a space no larger than a coffin. A fear of heights could lead to your soul perched miles up a cliff face. Maybe your idea of hell would be the torture inflicted by little demons."

"Little demons?" Kara repeated.

I looked around. "Chris isn't back yet."

"Probably fell asleep on the bed." Demarius laughed.

Ian Tremblin snatched a burning candle from the candelabrum, set it in the lantern, and passed it to me. "Will you please find our football star and bring him back?"

"Sure." The others started to discuss the qualities it takes to frighten readers as I went into the bedroom. The candle glow only revealed tones of gray and inky pools of shadow. To my left lay shards of glass from the picture that Chris had knocked off the wall. I squatted and looked at the painting. It was a nighttime rendition of Daemon Hall. The picture must have been painted in the winter because the surrounding trees were skeletal. A man stood a few paces from the front door gesturing toward the mansion. Both his hands were palm out, perhaps inviting someone inside. I could see color beyond low-light gray and looked closer. The man's hands were splashed with red. *Blood.*

Creepy picture.

I stood and saw a tall wardrobe against the opposite wall. The four-poster bed was empty. So much for the theory that Chris had fallen asleep.

"Chris," I called out.

No answer, but I did hear running water from a rectangle of black shadow, a doorway, across from the curtained window. I stepped with a splash and lowered the lantern to find water on the floor. I went through the door and saw a claw-foot bathtub against the far wall. Next to it was a full-length freestanding mirror. I stepped farther into the bathroom, splashing in quarter-inch-deep water. The toilet sat against the wall to my right. The large porcelain bowl sat on a narrow pedestal; both were painted with flowering vines. A hinged wooden seat leaned up against the wall. The tank was mounted to the wall just below the ceiling, connected to the bowl by a long, discolored pipe.

Over the running water, I heard a *glug*. Twin pedestal sinks painted with the same vine design were next to the toilet. The water came from the farthest, spilling over the basin onto the floor. I took a step toward it. The glugging sound came again. I took another step and saw movement beneath the running water in the flooded sink.

Glug.

Something wriggled in the sink.

Glug.

Another step closer, and I thought I was witnessing a scene from my own story.

Glug.

Was it a huge spider, waving its legs up from the basin? My heart pounded.

Glug.

The spider dropped an inch so that only the tips of its legs wiggled above water. I couldn't help myself and stepped closer.

Glug.

The spider limbs sank beneath the surface. At the sink, I raised the lantern.

Glug.

It wasn't a spider. Rising from the bottom of the sink was a hand, the wrist compacting and disappearing into the narrow drain.

Glug.

The drain swallowed more of the wrist. The movement caused the fingers to sway like seaweed. *Impossible,* was my one sane thought.

Glug-glug.

With a final tug of suction, the hand disappeared into the drain. I stared dumbly at the water swirling down the emptying sink, replaying in my mind how the bones and flesh contracted to fit into the drain and how the fingers had danced as they disappeared—as if waving good-bye.

I collapsed to my knees. Water soaked my pants. It was coming on. My eyes rolled back until I couldn't see. My heartbeat blasted, and I clutched my head, trying to squeeze out the pain. Too shallow, too fast, I thought, trying to control my breathing. I leaned forward until my head rested against the wet porcelain sink.

"Wade?"

Chelsea? And with her voice, the attack ended.

"Wade! Are you all right?"

"Yes—no—I mean—"

"Where are you? I'm coming in."

"No!" I shouted. It was dangerous. "No, don't. I'm coming out." I pulled myself up by the ravenous sink and backed out of the bathroom. Chelsea was silhouetted against the door leading into the study, and I stumbled past her.

She went into the bathroom—

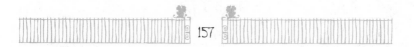

"Don't!"

—and returned a second later with the lantern. "Your pants are all wet."

"The water . . . spilled . . . on the bathroom floor. I—I fell." As I babbled, we returned to the study.

"Are you okay, Mr. Reilly?" Ian Tremblin said. "What happened?"

"Where's Chris?" Demarius asked.

"He disappeared down—" I began.

"He's gone?" Demarius said.

"That creep!" Chelsea shouted. "I knew he'd pull something like this."

"Huh?" They didn't understand.

"I knew he'd run off and hide. He's gonna jump out and scare us!"

"No!" They needed to know what happened to Chris. How could I put what I saw into words? The events reran in my head and seemed ludicrous. I mean, I'd only seen the hand for a second or two before it disappeared down the sink. *Seeing is believing?* That might be fine on a sunny day, but at night, in Daemon Hall, it could have been anything. A sane, rational mind would say that what I'd seen was physically impossible. My attack could've begun earlier than I thought, making me imagine it. It certainly wouldn't be out of character for Chris to go hide, waiting to scare everyone.

"Give me the lantern," Ian Tremblin said.

We trailed after the writer into the bedroom and then the bath-room. "He certainly made a mess," he said, and turned off the tap.

"But where is he?" Kara said.

"I think I can answer that." The writer strode back into the bedroom. "Over here, a door leads directly to the hall."

I hadn't seen the dark oak door in the shadow of the wardrobe. That explained it. I felt incredible relief. "Are you sure he's okay?"

"Maybe now," Chelsea growled. "But not when I get my hands on him. I don't care how many muscles he's got." Chelsea turned on her heels and stormed into the study.

"Should we look for him?" Demarius asked, trailing after her.

"No!" Chelsea snapped. "Maybe something in the dark will teach him a lesson."

Ian Tremblin sighed. "Well, as a minor, he is legally in my care. I'm not sure I should let him go stumbling around Daemon Hall at night. He could get injured."

"Serve him right," Chelsea mumbled.

"You could escort me out," Kara said. "On the way you could look for Chris."

"There you go, wanting to leave again," Demarius said. "We're halfway through the night. You might as well sit it out."

"No, she has a point, Demarius. This night is obviously not for her. We can escort her to the front gate, and in so doing, see if we can find our rebellious finalist."

"Thank you," Kara said.

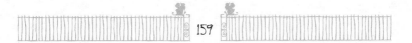

"But first, Kara," Ian Tremblin said, smiling, "I'd like for you to attempt a real story."

"What?" Kara asked.

"My young finalists, your entries were only a portion of the contest," Ian Tremblin said. "If you'll remember, another quality to be judged is storytelling."

"But we told stories," I pointed out.

"You *read* stories. What you have not done is to reach into your imagination, that fertile ground of the mind, to sow and tend the crop there and share it as it is harvested."

Demarius stared. "You mean we have to make up stories as part of the contest?"

"I can't do that," Kara said. "Not horror stories."

Ian Tremblin smiled. "The seeds of your stories were planted in your mind, who knows when, or by what circumstance. You need to nourish them with our surroundings. The general ambience of Daemon Hall should inspire your stories to grow surprisingly well. I promise, Kara, upon pain of death, that after your next story, the one you tell on the spot, you will be removed from our group."

"You shouldn't say you'll take her out and then change your mind," Chelsea said.

"He's not changing his mind. He said we'll escort her out after her made-up story," Demarius argued.

"That's right. It's simply time that we move on to the storytelling portion of our evening. I think Kara should be courteous enough to take part before she leaves."

"I can't make up stories like that," Kara pleaded.

"You can too." I was tired of her whining. "Give yourself some credit."

"Kara, as entertaining as your poem was, it wasn't really a story. Not like those from your fellow competitors, now was it? One of the reasons I selected you as a finalist is because your poem showed great imagination and potential, and I wondered what a story from you would be like. Won't you try? For me? For all of us?"

"What if I can't?"

"I tell you what. If you sincerely try and cannot do it, we will stop and aid in your escape. Is it a deal?" Ian Tremblin held out his hand.

"It's a deal," Kara whispered and shook his hand. "What do I do?"

"Stand there in front of the candelabrum. Here, place this candle back on it," he said, handing her the one from the lantern.

She shoved it into the vacant space. Three small flames burned.

"I don't know how to start," she said.

"*Once upon a time* has always been a popular way to kick a story into gear," Tremblin said, sitting high in his rigid chair.

Chelsea spoke to Kara. "In Stephen King's book *On Writing,* he likens storytelling to archaeology. He says that stories already exist and that as writers we have to use tools to uncover the story

bit by bit. The tools are theme, characters, description, dialogue; you get the idea. Like archaeologists, writers never really know what artifacts they'll dig up until they start."

"Artifacts?" Kara asked.

"There you go, dear. Something is coming to you, isn't it?"

"Archaeologists. Artifacts," Kara said. "Little demons."

"That's it, Kara. Let it come," Ian Tremblin droned.

"An anthropologist maybe? A professor? Her children. And—artifacts."

Artifacts

There were these two kids, a little older than me, about you guys' ages. The oldest, Ryan, was—um—he was sixteen. His sister, Tiffany, was younger, but only by a year. You know how a lot of brothers and sisters fight all the time, like my brother and me? Well, Ryan and Tiffany weren't like that. They were close. They hung out all the time. When Ryan needed help with schoolwork, Tiffany was always there. If Tiffany needed a ride, Ryan would drive her without any argument.

"Do they really make siblings like that?" Demarius asked, laughing.

"Be quiet," Chelsea said.

"Sorry."

They were real mature for being fifteen- and sixteen-year-olds. That was because their mom raised them to be independent, to look out for themselves as well as each other. It was necessary because their mother traveled all the time. She was an anthropologist and split her time between the classroom and being in the field conducting research. Their father—well—their father was dead. He'd gotten sick and died when they were real little.

They were good kids, with an exceptional mom, and a unique upbringing. And everything fell apart when their mother returned from one of her trips.

"I missed you guys. How were things while I was gone?"

"Just fine, Mom," Ryan said.

"I missed you." Tiffany hugged her mother.

"Well, I'm home now and don't foresee another trip soon," Professor Dowd said. "How about helping me with that?" She pointed out the open door to a three-foot-square wooden crate on the porch. The word *fragile,* written in half a dozen languages, had been stamped all over it. "You'll love the stuff I brought back."

It took all three of them to muscle the heavy crate down the hall and into Professor Dowd's office. Ryan ran to the garage and returned with a crowbar. Placing it under the lid of the box, he pushed down and worked it open.

"These artifacts were actually found southwest of Khoulada. I wouldn't be surprised if the city is thousands of years old. These pieces should give us an approximate date. We've nicknamed the new site Khoulada Two. It's hard to tell what it was like after so many centuries, but apparently the city was a collection of huts placed between three pyramids that served as the borders." Professor Dowd reached into the hay and shredded paper. She pulled out an ornately carved piece of wood. "You'll love this, Ryan," she said, showing him a large mask.

The face was long and thin, the lips drawn down in a fierce snarl with two tusks jutting up from the lower jaw and curving out toward the cheeks. The only painted features were the eyes: large white orbs traced in red. Long carved hair stood straight up.

"Cool!" Ryan said. "The Don King look."

"What's that, Mom?" Tiffany pointed to a curved dagger in the box. The knife had a rusted black blade and intricately sculpted stone grip.

"We think that may have been a sacrificial knife," she said, and gently placed the knife on her desk.

"They killed animals with it?"

"Not animals, Tiffany. Humans. And that's not rust on the blade."

"Oh, gross."

"Check it out," Ryan exclaimed, as his mother removed a long spearhead and shield from the crate. "They must have been fierce warriors."

"Maybe. We don't really know yet. These weapons are ceremonial. We found several in their temple." She carefully placed them on the floor. She spoke again, her voice dropping into a reverent whisper. "And these are the biggest puzzlers of all." Professor Dowd brought out a small figurine. It was made of dark wood and stood only ten inches high. As Ryan and Tiffany examined it, Professor Dowd brought out nine more and placed them on her table. "We have no idea what the significance is of these. I mentioned the temple. It's in the pyramid situated to the north of the city and stands three stories tall. Inside it are thousands of small recesses carved into the walls. They go from the floor all the way up to the pinnacle. Each niche has one of these small figures in it."

"They're ugly, Mom," Tiffany said.

The limbs of the figurines were long and malformed, like crude drawings of monsters made by children. Eyes, like those on the mask, glowered beneath low brows. Overlarge mouths, filled with needle teeth, gaped open. They wore carved loincloths. Each was a study in movement. Some looked like they were stalking and others attacking.

"Pretty gruesome," Ryan said.

"While they're all similar," their mother said, "they're all different. Each one has unique characteristics. You can almost see their own distinctive personalities."

"How many did you bring back?" Ryan asked.

"Just these ten."

"Khoulada is located in the highlands just over the Guinea border from the northwest part of the Ivory Coast," Professor Dowd told her class.

As was often the case when she returned from her trips, Ryan and Tiffany sat in the back during her late-afternoon class, learning the anthropological specifics of what their mother had been up to during her travels.

"Khoulada is a newly discovered village, which has been kept hidden from modern man until Dr. Moriega stumbled onto it while researching medicinal plants from that region. The topography of high-reaching cliffs made a natural hideaway for Khoulada. However, it's even more difficult traveling to the deserted city we've nicknamed Khoulada Two. After climbing the cliffs, we then had to travel over four miles through underground tunnels before emerging into the Khoulada Two valley.

"The deserted city is shrouded in mystery. Where did the people go? Why did they go? And these intriguing questions— what are these figurines, and what is their purpose?"

"Cool," Ryan whispered to Tiffany. "She brought the statues with her."

Professor Dowd lined up the figurines on the lectern in front of her. "The temple had thousands of these. I only brought back a sample of ten figures and—and— That's peculiar." Professor Dowd stopped her monologue. She looked carefully into the canvas bag she brought them in. "I'm sorry. Apparently, I only brought nine of the figurines. As you file by, please refrain from touching them. We can't even begin to put a price on their value."

Ryan and Tiffany lingered after class.

"Is there anything you would like to tell me?" Professor Dowd asked sternly as she put the figurines back into the bag.

"Like what, Mom?" Tiffany asked.

"Like, where is the tenth Khoulada Two figurine?"

"You don't think we did something with it, do you? I mean, Tiffany can't stand them, and I'm not sure I like having them around the house either."

Their mom's expression melted into a contrite smile. "I'm sorry. It's just odd. I remember loading them into this bag and counting ten as I did so."

Back at home Ryan and Tiffany went into the kitchen for a snack while their mother went to her office. Half an hour later she called for them.

Ryan saw the desperate look on her face. "Jeez, Mom, what's up?"

"You still haven't found it?" Tiffany asked.

"No, and this will be big trouble. These artifacts are on loan from the government of Guinea. I had to fill out a mountain of paperwork just to get them out of the country. This could affect future projects for us in that region. I'm sure I'll be held accountable."

"Come on," Ryan said. "We'll help you look for it."

They spent the next hour looking through the office and searching the house.

"Where is it?" Professor Dowd fell into her desk chair. "Am I going insane? I had ten, right?"

"Yeah, Mom. We saw them," Ryan said.

"Was it stolen? Did I misplace it?" Her voice rose in frustration and she slammed her hand onto her desk. "Dammit! Where is it?"

Ryan and Tiffany stared wide-eyed. They'd never seen their mother so frantic.

Professor Dowd shook her head and sighed. "You two better leave me alone. I have to call the dean and report this. It's not going to be pleasant."

An hour later Professor Dowd walked into the living room where Ryan was on the computer and Tiffany sat reading a book.

Tiffany looked up and asked, "How'd it go?"

"About as bad as I expected. There's an emergency meeting first thing tomorrow morning. The dean wants to wait until he discusses it with campus security before he brings in the police. I've locked the remaining nine figurines in my display case. So there's nothing more we can do about it now. Oh my, look at the time. Why don't you two help me get dinner started."

During their meal the professor told them about her latest expedition. How they took small boats up a river and how an angry hippopotamus had attacked her boat, nearly knocking her into the water. Throughout her narration, Ryan and Tiffany could hear the stress in her voice.

She yawned and stretched. "Well, this old world traveler is ready for bed. Get your homework done before you turn on the TV and make sure you lock up."

⟨⟩

Tiffany switched off the TV as a *Buffy the Vampire Slayer* rerun ended. They went from room to room and shut off lights before taking the wide, carpeted staircase up to the second floor. As they reached the landing, they both froze at the sound of breaking glass.

"Did you hear that, Ryan? It came from downstairs," Tiffany whispered.

"Shhh, listen a minute!"

"Let's get Mom," Tiffany said.

"Naw, she's exhausted. We can handle this."

"What if someone's breaking in?"

"Here," Ryan said, picking up the cordless phone and handing it to her. "You follow behind me and get ready to call 9-1-1."

Agreeing to check the kitchen first, they cautiously made their way downstairs and into the hallway, turning on lights as they went. As they passed the closed door of their mother's office, they heard a thump.

"In there," Ryan said in an urgent whisper.

"Let's get Mom. Please."

"In a minute. C'mon." Ryan turned the doorknob. Taking a

deep breath, he shoved the door open and turned on the light. No one was there. "Neither of the windows is broken. The noise must have come from somewhere else."

"No," Tiffany said, her voice trembling. "There's the broken glass."

She pointed to the bottom corner of their mother's display case. Several shards of glass lay underneath it. Above the broken glass, on the first shelf, were the Khoulada Two figurines—all ten of them.

Ryan and Tiffany woke their mother, and she called the police. It was her opinion that they were victims of a prank, a sick joke of sorts. Ryan and Tiffany thought that it may have had something to do with the figurines themselves.

"What? Supernatural? Little demons running around?" Professor Dowd asked.

"Come on, Mom, you have to admit they're pretty weird, and you already said that you don't know what they are," Ryan said.

"They're creepy, Mom," Tiffany added.

"I don't believe this! I have raised you to be rational, reasoning, and scientific. And here you are talking about bogeymen!"

"Mom!"

Professor Dowd took a deep breath. "I've been a veritable crank, haven't I? I tell you what; I'll take them to the college tomorrow and keep them there. Will that do?"

"Yes," Tiffany sighed.

"Let's get to bed. The police said they'd drive by a few times tonight. I'll make an appointment tomorrow to have all our locks changed. As for the figurines, they really are just little statues. Someone played a joke on us, that's all, tried to scare us."

"They did a good job," Ryan said.

❁

The next morning Ryan woke as Tiffany shook his shoulder.

"Get up, Ryan. Mom's going out of the country again."

"Wha'? Whaddya mean?" Ryan mumbled. "She just got back."

"I know, but she's leaving again."

Ryan climbed from bed and went hastily through his morning routine. He ran down the stairs and found his mom and sister, both looking anxious, at the kitchen table. Tiffany pushed a bowl of cereal and a carton of milk in front of his chair.

"What's going on?" he asked. "Tiff said you're leaving again."

"Yes. I'm so sorry, but it's an emergency."

"What emergency?"

"I received a call early this morning. There's been trouble at the Khoulada Two site."

"What kind of trouble?" Ryan asked.

"I'm not sure. That's why I have to go. They need someone who's familiar with the site and who isn't, well, superstitious."

"You're scaring me, Mom," Tiffany said.

"I truly don't know what's going on. The company that organizes our expeditions called and said everyone at Khoulada Two has vanished. Locals are claiming it's bad juju. They won't mount a search. That's why I have to go. Dr. Zawinul, three graduate students, and eight laborers are missing. I have to help find out what happened to them."

"You?" Tiffany exclaimed. "It sounds like something the police should handle, not a professor."

"Tiffany, honey, Khoulada Two is in the middle of nowhere. There aren't any police to look into it. But I'm sure the Guinea government will supply soldiers to accompany us."

"Don't go, Mom," Tiffany pleaded.

"Yeah, don't go," Ryan added. "It could be dangerous."

"I have to go, I'm sorry. I'm sure there's a reasonable explanation. Please don't worry."

"What about us, Mom? Someone was in the house last night," Tiffany said.

"I've called a locksmith. He'll come change the locks later today. Mr. Radiman from next door has promised to look in on you from time to time. Campus security said they will patrol regularly out here until I get back. I've even talked to Gabriel's mother and she's agreed that if you guys get uncomfortable here by yourselves, Tiffany can stay with them. And Ryan, I'm sure Adam's mother would let you stay at their house. So there you go, it's all taken care of."

"What about the figurines, Mom?" Tiffany asked. "Will you take them with you?"

Professor Dowd frowned. "To be honest, I forgot. I suppose I can call Grant and see if he'll pick them up."

"Don't forget," Tiffany said.

On her way to the airport, Professor Dowd made a mental check-list of things to do while waiting for her flight. Calling Grant to pick up the figurines was last on the list. She got around to calling minutes before her flight departed, but his line was busy. *I'll call him from New York,* she thought. Once on the plane, she opened her laptop and began to go over her notes. By the time they landed in New York, where she would board her flight to Africa, she had forgotten Grant altogether.

Shortly after Ryan and Tiffany got home from school, the lock-smith arrived and put in new locks. "Here are the keys," he said, and handed them to Ryan.

"Thanks."

"I wonder when Grant is coming to pick up the little demons," Tiffany said as she closed the door behind the locksmith.

"If Mom heard you call them demons you'd be in for one of her rational-mind lectures."

"I call them as I see them. Those things are small and evil; therefore, it only makes sense to refer to them as little demons. How's that for rational thought?"

"I bow to your excellent logic," Ryan said, and genuflected out of the entryway.

"Where are you going?"

"I want to look at those little demons again, make sure they're all there."

Tiffany followed him into the office. They stood in front of the glass case. Professor Dowd had covered the small break with cardboard and duct tape.

Ryan dragged his index finger across the glass as he counted them. "Ten little demons all present and accounted for."

"Do they look different to you?" Tiffany asked.

"What do you mean?"

"They just look different, like they're in different positions. And I don't remember any of them with weapons."

"Weapons?"

Tiffany pointed. Two of the figurines held items. One clasped a tiny spear. The second held a knife that was a miniature of the one their mother had brought back.

"Man, oh, man," Ryan said. "I don't remember that. I hope Grant comes soon."

They waited until nine, then looked up Grant's phone number in their mother's Rolodex and phoned him. His roommate answered and said Grant would be out most of the evening. Ryan left a message.

"I guess Mom forgot to call Grant. Oh, well," Ryan said. "One more night with the ten little bogeymen won't hurt us."

"I don't like it, Ry. Those things really creep me out."

"Come on, Tiff, don't get freaked. I mean, what do we know about them? One disappeared and then was placed back in Mom's office. Creepy, yeah. Logically, though, do you really think it scampered off and then returned by itself?"

"Not really. But how about those two with the weapons?"

"We didn't notice they had them until today, that's all."

"Would it be all right if I stayed in your room tonight?"

Ryan grinned at his sister. "Gee, it's been a long time since you've wanted to have a sleepover. Aren't you a little old?" She answered him with a punch on his arm. "Ouch! Okay, do you want the bottom bunk or top?"

"I'll take the top. It'll be a harder climb for itty-bitty demons."

"You know, I'd think that was funnier if they weren't down the hall."

⚜

Just past eleven that night, as they watched a Reese Witherspoon comedy, Grant called. Ryan explained about the artifacts.

"No problem," Grant said. "I'll pick them up first thing in the morning."

"Come on in if we're not here. We'll put a spare key in the usual place."

"Sure thing. Are you guys okay by yourselves?"

"We're fine."

After the movie, Ryan and Tiffany put on their pajamas and got ready for bed. Tiffany climbed up on the top bunk, and Ryan reclined below. Just like years earlier, when they'd have regular sleepovers, they spent a long time talking in the dark, though they purposefully avoided any topics having to do with anthropological artifacts. When the conversation lagged, Ryan and Tiffany fell asleep.

"Ryan! Wake up!" An urgent whisper.

Wiping his eyes, Ryan glanced at the phosphorescent hands of his wind-up alarm clock. "It's three fifteen, Tiff."

"Ryan! Something's in the room!"

Ryan sat up and listened. Something small scuttled along the floor next to the far wall. He instinctively reached for his bedside lamp, but it didn't work.

"Turn on a light, Ry!" Tiffany whispered.

"I'm trying. My lamp burned a bulb. Just a minute."

In the darkness, Ryan wrestled from under the covers and made his way over the hardwood floor to the light switch on the wall.

"It's not working, Tiff! The power must be—*ouch!*"

"Ryan, what happened?"

"Something just—I mean my—*ow!* Something is stabbing my foot!"

Tiffany shrieked as Ryan ran back to the bunk beds and climbed on top with her.

"I think I'm bleeding," Ryan said, clearly frightened.

They sat in the dark and heard the noise again. Only now it sounded as if there were more of them running along the floor.

"My flashlight!" Ryan whispered.

"Where?"

"It's in the top drawer of my desk, I can lean over and get it without getting off the bed."

"Be careful."

Tiffany felt the bed shake as Ryan positioned himself and leaned off the bed. She heard the muted wood-on-wood squeak of his desk drawer opening. As he blindly rummaged through the drawer, she heard the floor-sound change. They were heading toward them!

"Hurry, Ryan! They're coming!"

"Got it!" he said.

"Turn it on!"

Ryan clicked on the flashlight.

Tiffany screamed.

⚜

The phone rang.

"Hello," Grant said. "Professor Dowd's residence."

"This is Professor Dowd, who is this?"

"Hey, Professor. It's Grant."

"What's wrong, Grant?"

"Everything's fine, Professor. I just came over to pick up the artifacts."

"Oh, thank you. With everything going on I forgot to contact you."

"Yeah, we figured that. I spoke with Ryan last night and came over this morning."

"I hope you don't mind doing this. Ryan and Tiffany felt uncomfortable having them in the house."

"No problem."

"Can I speak with them?"

"They aren't here, Professor. Ryan said they might be gone and left the key for me in the planter."

"Leave a note to let them know I phoned."

"Sure. When do you get to Khoulada Two?"

"Not soon enough."

"Let us know when you learn what happened."

"I will, Grant. Are you on the kitchen phone or office phone?"

"I'm right here in your office. I just opened the case and was getting set to put the figurines in my bag."

"Do me a favor and count them. We had an incident where one went missing for a short while. Are they all there?"

"I guess so. Just a minute, let me check."

Grant quietly counted the figurines and returned to the phone. "Okay, one dozen all accounted for."

". . . Excuse me, Grant, how many?"

"Twelve."

"But I only— Are you positive?"

"Yes, I'm sure there are twelve. It's kinda weird. You know how most of them have loincloths? If I didn't know any better, I'd say two of them are wearing pajamas. Isn't that funny? Hello, Professor, are you still there? Professor Dowd—hello—hello?"

Y̶ou made up that awesome story? Our little scaredy-cat Kara?" Demarius asked.

Behind her thick glasses, Kara's eyes were vacant.

"I didn't know you had it in you, Kara," I praised her.

She blinked quickly several times. "In me?"

"Yeah, the story you just told. I didn't know you had it in you."

"Is in me?"

"Kara?" Chelsea said. "Are you all right?"

"In me?" Kara screamed and jumped into motion. She ran toward the door but stopped before she left the candlelight. She turned and ran right past me toward the bedroom suite, but again stopped without leaving the light. Finally, she launched herself at the sofa and sobbed into the cushions.

"What's wrong?" Demarius said. "That was a great story. Why are you crying?"

Demarius and I exchanged glances. Chelsea knelt by Kara and whispered something to her.

"Boys," Ian Tremblin said, "let's see if Chris has returned to the suite and let the ladies sort this out." At the bedroom he called out, "Chris! Olly-olly-oxen-free!"

Hushed whimpers and a whispered discussion from the sofa were the only sounds.

"I suppose Chris is still enjoying himself," Tremblin said.

We stood in uncomfortable silence, glancing occasionally at Kara and Chelsea. "I can't . . . a mistake . . . I didn't . . ." Snatches of what Kara said drifted our way.

"Say, Mr. Tremblin, what's up with Kara?" Demarius whispered, nodding in her direction.

"Oh, I imagine it's what Wade said."

"What I said?" I looked back and saw how upset she was. "I didn't say anything. Did I?"

Ian Tremblin smiled. "You said 'I didn't know you had it in you.' It upset her."

"Why? I didn't mean anything by it."

"Because prior to tonight, all those things that she found frightening were not a part of her, or so she thought," Tremblin

explained. "They were outside of her, these movies, stories, and books that frightened her. Since she didn't want any part of them, she could always turn away, turn it off, ignore it, or go elsewhere. But as you inadvertently pointed out, Wade, that story came from within her. It's *in* her. There's no escaping what's in you. Now she worries about what else is within her."

"I want to go now. I really, really want to go," Kara called to Ian Tremblin. "Call me a coward if you want, but I am ready to leave."

"No one is calling you a coward, Miss Bakshi. You've already demonstrated a great deal of courage by showing up, even if it was because of the bullying of your brother and mother. Extinguish your candle, Kara, and we'll leave."

Kara approached the candelabrum on shaky legs and swatted the lowest burning candle. Melted wax flew as she crushed the flame.

Ian Tremblin walked to her and placed a hand on her shoulder. "It's time." Of the two candles still burning, he took one to place in his lantern.

We navigated the warren of hallways and reached the marble staircase. All of us stopped and watched the writer descend. From the top of the stairs, looking down, the entry hall seemed more like a massive cavern than a man-made structure. The farther he got from us, the bleaker it became. After a moment, we rushed to catch up and stay within the protective lantern light.

"Man, this place is huge," Demarius said at the bottom of the stairs.

"If you want an example of the sheer magnitude of the house, follow me," Ian Tremblin said, turning right.

"Where are you going, Mr. Tremblin?" Kara said. "We came in the other way."

"A quick detour, if you please," he said. "I want to show you something."

Kara glanced toward the distant front door, then followed.

"Here we are, at the head of a hallway that leads into the east wing. Look down the hallway and tell me what you see."

Chelsea, Demarius, and I stepped forward and peered into the dark. Kara stood close behind me.

"What is it?" Chelsea asked.

I couldn't see anything at first, then, in the blackness, I saw the tiniest pinprick of light.

"I think I see something." Demarius squinted.

"At the end of this hall is a floor-to-ceiling mirror. Mrs. Daemon was fond of mirrors. What you see is the reflection from my lantern."

"Man, that is one long hallway," Demarius said.

"And totally unneeded." The author walked to twin doors that opened to a dark chamber. "All the rooms lining this side of the hallway are interconnected. Here's a parlor. There's also a library, a sitting room, a sunroom, a den, an office, and a servant's bedroom. Each is connected by a door that opens into the next room, like adjoining hotel rooms."

"Can we leave, please?" Kara asked.

"Just a minute," Demarius said. "Do that thing with the lantern and mirror again."

"We'll get you out in a minute," I told Kara as we stood by the parlor door, and then went to join the others at the hallway.

When I noticed she didn't follow, I looked back, and reality shifted into slow motion. Kara, merely ten feet from us, no longer stood in front of open double doors, a dark room behind her. It looked as if she was floating on a pool of black water. Something stirred just below the surface. A form in the black water slowly took shape as a grinning face appeared over Kara's shoulder. Fear struck me like a jolt of electricity. An arm broke through the black surface. At the shock on my face, Kara turned to see what I saw. The mad face leered at me. The arm, violently scarred from biceps to wrist, wrapped around Kara's waist. She opened her mouth to scream, but I could only hear my rushing blood. Yanked into the black water, she disappeared.

Time flow returned to normal. The parlor doors slammed. Kara's screams diminished as she was pulled deeper into the house, doors closing after her. A malignant silence followed the last, distant report of a slamming door.

"Did you see? Did you see? Man, oh, man! It looked like something sucked her into that room." Demarius pointed, his voice cracking.

"Come on!" Chelsea shouted, and ran to the door.

I tried the next door down the hallway, and Demarius the one after that. We twisted the knobs, pulled and pushed, but the doors wouldn't open.

Chelsea rushed back to Ian Tremblin. "We need tools. Do you have a crowbar or something like that, Mr. Tremblin?"

"Oh, my," he spoke, eyes unfocused.

"Mr. Tremblin! A crowbar?" Demarius shouted.

"No, no tools," the writer said, sounding almost asleep.

"You must have tools, maybe in your car?" Chelsea pleaded.

"Perhaps my driver—" Ian Tremblin answered in a faraway voice.

"Do you have a cell phone, Mr. Tremblin? We can call for help."

"No, a phone is against the rules," he said.

"We've got to find her, Mr. Tremblin. Snap out of it!" Chelsea demanded.

Ian Tremblin's eyes were enormous. "Are you sure it wasn't Chris who—who grabbed Kara? Chris having his fun?"

I shook my head and felt like sobbing. "No it wasn't! I saw him! The guy who grabbed her was—was crazy. He had a scar, a long scar on his arm, like—the man—the psycho in Chelsea's babysitter story."

Chelsea turned from the parlor doors. "Maybe Chris didn't run off."

"I saw what happened to Chris," I admitted, clutching at my temples. "At least, I think I did. I thought I was seeing things, but now, after this . . . in the bathroom—in the sink."

Ian Tremblin grabbed me by the shoulders. "What did you see?"

"Chris's hand, in the sink. His wrist in the drain. It was sucked down."

"In the sink? That's not possible," Chelsea said.

Angry, I pulled free from Ian Tremblin's grip. "Don't you think I know that? But I saw it just the same!"

"I'm beginning to think anything is possible in this house," Ian Tremblin said, and narrowed his black eyes. "We need to get out of Daemon Hall."

Chelsea jabbed a finger in his chest. "We can't just leave Kara!"

"I'm responsible for all of you, not just Kara. We need to leave—to get to the front gate and my driver. We'll call the police, and they'll find Kara and Chris. Let's go."

We didn't need much convincing.

"*Five little finalists waiting at the door—one vanished down a hole and then there were four,*" Ian Tremblin said as we rushed for the exit. "*Four little finalists plain for all to see—one was dragged into the night and then there were three.*"

"Shut up, Mr. Tremblin! Just shut up!" Chelsea screamed at him. "Do you think your little poem is funny now?"

Ian Tremblin looked back at her, shocked. "Not at all, my dear. I didn't mean to seem crass, I'm just thinking out loud. That poem and what's happening, there seems to be a connection."

"Where did that poem come from, Mr. Tremblin?" Demarius asked.

"It just came to me out there by the gate. I thought I was inspired by your recitation of 'Ten Little Indians.'"

"Chris and Kara disappeared exactly like the first two in that poem," I said. "Chris went down a hole: the drain. And someone dragged Kara into the dark."

"*Three little finalists made up this hearty crew—one was forced to walk the plank and then there were two,*" Ian Tremblin continued. "*Two little finalists, one went on the run—screamed and tripped and broke a neck and then there was one. The last little finalist almost had it won—that finalist went insane and then there were none.*"

The marble entryway seemed much longer on the way out than coming in. I had the feeling that something moved parallel to us, just out of the lantern's reach.

"Here we are." Ian Tremblin handed the lantern to Demarius and grabbed the doorknob, but it wouldn't turn. "No, it can't be—"

"Get out of the way." Chelsea shouldered the writer aside. She tried twisting the knob. "Is it locked?"

Ian Tremblin fished in a jacket pocket and retrieved an antique key. He placed it in the lock, but like the knob, it wouldn't budge. "The house won't let us leave."

"The hell it won't," Chelsea snarled. She grabbed the nearest covered chair, ripped off the sheet, and picked it up by its spindle-back. She slung it two-handed at a window and was rewarded with the sound of shattering glass. She smiled at us, then another crash followed as thick wooden shutters closed over the broken window.

Ian Tremblin took the candle from the lantern and replaced it on the candelabrum. Returning to the familiar study brought no comfort.

"I can't believe we came back up here," Chelsea said.

"We tried every door, every window." Demarius shook his head.

"There's only one conclusion," Ian Tremblin said. "The house wants us to stay."

"How long?" Demarius asked.

"Perhaps after the tenth story Daemon Hall will allow us to go." I fell into my chair. Demarius and Ian Tremblin sat.

"Maybe that's your conclusion." Chelsea paced by the candles. "I have another."

"And what is that, Chelsea?"

"All this could have been arranged by you. It's just like something from one of your books. The strange things, the missing people could be your version of Fear Factor. That makes more sense than an evil house craving ghost stories."

"Chelsea, I assure you—"

"Just answer my question," Chelsea shouted. "Are there other people here, with wind machines and special effects? Are there actors, pretending to be psycho killers or ghosts or whatever? Give me a straight answer, or I'll go see for myself!"

Ian Tremblin shook his head. "I reiterate that I believe the house has us in its possession until the last tale. I suggest we resume the ancient art of storytelling."

The three of us glanced at one another.

Chelsea stepped in front of the candelabrum and stared at the two burning candles. After a deep breath, she began. "There's this couple. They've been together for almost a year. They think it's true love. The guy has been pressuring her for sex. He's not being a jerk. He simply thinks they're ready. Are they? Is she? That's not up to me, I'm just the storyteller. There is one thing I know she's not ready for, one thing she would never willingly give: an invitation."

Invitation

Didn't you say the lake would be busy this weekend?" the girlfriend asks. Her name is Alysa.

Her boyfriend is named Jay, and he tells her, "Usually there's a ton of boats out, lots of fishermen and water skiers."

Jay and Alysa are on a deck next to a porch swing. The white clapboard cabin, tinged green by the fungus that grows in the humid air, perches high on a wooded hill overlooking a large lake. At least fifty other cabins are visible from where they stand.

"Come on, let's get inside before anyone sees us," Jay says, unlocking the door.

"Can't we sit on the swing first?" Alysa asks in a little-girl voice.

Jay laughs. "After dark, when no one can see us, we'll come out and swing away."

"Promise?"

"Promise."

She walks past the large lake-facing window and follows Jay inside. Alysa knows his mood from the spark in his eyes. She feels the same. He takes her in his arms and kisses her. Alysa returns the affection, but stops after a time.

"Not now, Romeo." She laughs and pulls away.

"Awww."

"God, it stinks in here. Smells like a litter box."

Jay sniffs. "It's the moisture. Everything gets musty. We'll open some windows after dark and air it out."

"Can't we open them now? Do you really think anyone will notice?"

"Probably. And then there'll be someone at the door wanting to crack a beer with Dad or gossip with Mom. If we get caught, you can bet our folks will hear about it. Do you want to tell your dad why we're spending the night together?"

"Oh, yeah. Gosh, Daddy, I know I told you I was staying over at Sara's house, but I thought a pillow fight with Jay would be more fun."

"Your father would kill me." Jay laughs.

"The cabin stinks," Alysa repeats, looking around the small den. A couple of cheap prints hang in equally cheap frames on the wood-paneled walls. Mismatched stuffed chairs face a lumpy brown sofa across from a scarred coffee table. "Can we open one window?"

Jay nods. He leads her through a doorway into a tiny kitchen outfitted with ancient appliances. He unlocks a window above the sink and wiggles it back and forth until it finally slides up, and he props it open with a piece of wood.

"This window faces the woods. No one will notice."

Jay takes Alysa on a tour of the cabin. A skinny door in the living room opens onto a bathroom. "Granpop and Dad added it on. Before that there was an outhouse."

"You mean this isn't an outhouse? It's about as big," Alysa says with a smile.

"And now to the bedroom suite of our four-star accommodations," Jay says.

He takes her hand, and they cross the living room to an iron spiral staircase in the corner. Alysa tightens her grip on Jay's hand as they climb, uneasy on the shaky stairs. The bedroom is a low-ceilinged loft overcrowded with a queen-size bed and two end tables.

"Oooh, nice bed," Alysa purrs, taking Jay's arm. "Where are you going to sleep?"

"What?"

Laughing, Alysa runs down the stairs with Jay close behind her. She kneels in front of the large window that looks out on the lake and pulls the curtains aside. Jay sits beside her and opens the window a few inches.

"Thanks," she says, and takes a deep breath of fresh air. "It really is a beautiful lake, even if it is crowded with cabins."

"My grandfather was the first person to build here. He said it was really peaceful, then other people began to build until it's like you see now. It's jammin' in the summer."

"Yeah, jammin'. It's more like a ghost town," Alysa says.

"I guarantee you that people are in almost all the cabins. I know for a fact that Derek is here. They were coming up today, just like us."

"Derek Caine?"

Jay points out the window to the left. "His folks' cabin is the second one down."

"You didn't tell him we were coming, did you?"

"The way that guy blabs? Our getaway is a secret, unless you told someone."

"Who would I tell?"

"Meagan."

"No way. She talks as much as Derek. The only people who know we're at your parents' cabin are you and me."

"My cabin," Jay says.

"What?"

"My cabin. You said it was my parents' cabin, but it's mine."

"What are you talking about?"

"Granpop left it to me in his will. So technically it's mine."

"Really? I mean it's not much, but I didn't know you owned it. You're a land baron."

Jay laughs.

"Still, it's *your* cabin." Alysa looks intently at Jay. "*Your* place. I like that. It makes me more comfortable about being here."

They sit before the den window all afternoon and talk. When the sky darkens and they're sure they won't be seen, they go outside. The chains on the porch swing groan softly as they sit. Small talk turns to comfortable silence. They hold hands, then hold each other, and then kiss.

A piercing sound echoes to the lake and back.

"What was that?" Alysa asks.

"I don't know." Jay shrugs. "An animal, I guess."

"It sounded like a scream," Alysa whispers.

"Nah, it was an animal," Jay says, and moves in for another kiss. Alysa holds him back and looks into the dark night.

The sound repeats, louder this time. Jay stands. The only visible light comes from Derek Caine's family cabin. The scream starts again but abruptly dies.

Alysa stands behind Jay, her breath loud and shaky. "What do you—"

"Shhh," Jay whispers.

There's movement by Derek's cabin. It's too far to make out, but several people move in front of the cabin light. The light extinguishes.

"Let's go in," Jay whispers.

"I'm scared," Alysa says.

Jay locks the door and peeks out the window. "I don't think anything is really wrong, but—" He drops the curtain back into place.

"But what?"

"It's just weird. None of the cabins have their lights on. No one was at the lake today. That scream."

"Maybe we should leave."

"We don't have enough money for a motel. We'd have to sit in the car all night."

"Should we call the police?"

"I don't know. Maybe. If something is really wrong. On the other hand, we'll get caught for sure if we call the police." Jay turns on a table lamp.

"Well, what should we do?" Alysa asks, pacing the small room.

"I'll call Derek at his cabin. See what's going on."

"Don't tell him we're here."

"I won't. I'll pretend we're still in town, just checking to see what's happening at the lake. Give me the phone." Jay holds out his hand.

"What?"

"Give me the cell phone."

"I don't have it."

"You used it to call your mom and tell her you were staying at Sara's, remember?"

"It must still be in the car. Isn't there a phone here?"

"No. Dad says what's the point of getting away if you can be reached by phone."

"So now what?"

"I guess I'll go get the phone."

"But we parked way back by the road."

"I didn't want anyone seeing the car. It'll only take me about fifteen minutes, quicker if I hurry."

"I'm not sure it's such a good idea," Alysa says.

"I'll be careful."

"Do you want me to come with you?"

"Do you want to come with me?"

"Not really."

"Then stay here. I'll be right back." Jay goes into the kitchen and returns with a large flashlight. "Don't turn on too many lights. Lock the door behind me. Don't open it for anyone but me."

"How will I know it's you?"

"I'll give you a secret knock. How about the ol' 'shave and a haircut—two bits'?" He knocks on the doorjamb. *Bam-bam-be-bam-bam*—pause—*bam-bam.*

Alysa walks to him and puts her left arm around his waist. "You're a favorite customer. I won't charge you two bits. The shave and a haircut is on the house." *Bam-bam-be-bam-bam,* she knocks on the jamb.

Jay kisses her and slips out the door. Alysa locks it after he leaves and goes into the kitchen to watch him through the woods-facing window. When the flashlight beam disappears among the trees, she closes the window and returns to the living room. There are a number of dusty Reader's Digest condensed books on a shelf. She picks one and sits on the couch. She thumbs through it for a few minutes and then remembers the den window is cracked open. Alysa crosses the room and closes it. She begins pacing.

How long has he been gone? she wonders. *Five minutes, maybe? That leaves ten minutes or so until he's back.* She checks her watch. Her breath catches as she hears something skitter across the deck. *It was just a squirrel or a raccoon,* she decides. The scare leaves a funny feeling in her gut. She has to pee and goes to the bathroom. She comes out and checks her watch again. Seven minutes to go. She sits on the sofa and opens the book. She forces herself not to look at her watch. After trying to read a couple more pages, she gives up and glances at her wrist. Only four more minutes have passed?

She goes up the stairs and turns down the covers on the bed. She turns on both end-table lamps, not caring how much light they produce. She checks her watch again. Three more minutes have passed. She sits on the bed. Her gaze returns to her watch. The two lamps in the loft and the one downstairs go out. Everything disappears in darkness. Jay is late.

Alysa stands. She shuffles to the loft railing and peers blindly below, losing herself in the act of listening for Jay's return. Outside, the moon rises, providing a barely noticeable luminosity that shines through the sides of the den window drapes. Black gives way to grays. The furnishings below take shape. She's been in the loft for a long time, maybe half an hour.

Trying to be as quiet as possible, she descends the spiral staircase. She starts for the cramped kitchen, but stops when there's a knock at the door. *Bam-bam-be-bam-bam.*

"Jay!" She rushes to the door and reaches for the knob.

The knock continues. *Bam-bam!*

Instant terror takes her past being startled and into momentary paralysis. That wasn't the knock they agreed on. An inch at a time, she withdraws her hand.

Bam-bam-be-bam-bam!

"Shave and a haircut," she sings in a trembling whisper. "But no two bits, remember? Shave and a haircut, that's all."

Bam-bam!

"Shave and a haircut," Alysa chants, her mind clouding.

Bam-bam-be-bam-bam!

"Shave and a haircut—that's all."

Bam-bam!

"No two bits!" she screams.

Bam-bam-be-bam-bam!

"Stop it—now!"

Bam-bam!

"No!" Without conscious thought, she throws open the door.

People are in front of the cabin. Some stand in the dim moonlight. Others perch in the limbs of trees. Some, impossibly so, seem to drift in the night breeze. Thirty, forty, maybe more. They all watch

Alysa with blank faces. Some wear swimsuits. More than a few wear pajamas. Vacant-faced children in cutoffs and T-shirts are scattered among the grown-ups. There are men in Bermuda shorts and Hawaiian shirts and women in summer dresses. A tall man stands in front of them. He wears a black suit, and his arms dangle well past the ends of his sleeves. Alysa dazedly sees that the coat isn't too small, but the man's arms are too long. His head is completely hairless and his eyes are wide, staring at her in childlike wonder. His pale, thin lips move into a smile, accentuating two long teeth that extend from his mouth and fit into holes in his chin. The man opens his mouth, and the teeth lift from the punctures, yet no blood trickles. He closes his mouth, and his teeth return to their fleshy pockets.

Invitation?

Alysa hears the word in her head.

Invitation?

Somehow she knows the one-word question comes from the black-dressed man.

Invitation?

Her attention is drawn to his eyes. They are so innocent. Alysa, for the first time since she heard the screams, feels at peace.

Invitation?

And longing. There is something desirable about him.

Invitation?

Hadn't she come up to this stinky little cabin for romance? What could be more romantic than inviting him in, inviting all of them, and giving herself up to them?

Invitation?

Yes. All she has to do is stand aside and invite them in. It will be so romantic, so erotic, so very—so very . . . deadly.

Alysa screams and slams the door. She shakes her head, trying to clear the strange man's thoughts from her mind. The man's influence fades, and she realizes he almost manipulated her into offering an invitation inside. She races upstairs, the rickety staircase swinging from side to side. Looking for a safe spot, she squeezes into a corner by the farthest end table. She pushes against the wall, forcing herself deeper into the little recess.

She hears a rattle and a click. What is that? The doorknob! In her panic she had not locked it! The door squeaks open, is silent a moment, and squeaks closed. Footsteps. Someone walks into the downstairs room and stops. Unable to stop shaking, she waits. She has been so patient, waiting for Jay to return and now waiting for that evil man to resume his trek across the floor and up the staircase. She's tired of waiting.

"No!" Alysa screams and jumps up. She runs for the loft railing, leans over, and yells. "You don't have an invitation! You can't come in!"

"It's my cabin. I don't need an invitation."

Alysa blinks, not believing. Jay stands there, barely visible in the center of the dark den. He looks up at Alysa and smiles.

"Jay? Is that really you?"

"I'm back," he says, and starts up the spiral staircase.

"Don't invite them in," she says. Her voice sounds like a frightened child's. "They can't come in without an invitation."

"No. I won't invite them in," he says softly, reaching for her. "If I did, I'd have to share you."

He takes her in his arms and kills her with a kiss.

Ian Tremblin's face was hidden in shadow. "Interesting theme. Betrayed by someone you love. Not much confidence in relationships, eh? Why is that, I wonder?"

"Experience," Chelsea mumbled, and blew out a candle.

Only one remained.

I heard a scurrying sound, and Demarius gasped. It came again, just out of candlelight near the fireplace. Staring into the darkness, I moved to Chelsea's side. It scrabbled like fingernails scraping the wall. Another scampering began across the room. Ian Tremblin glanced wildly around as he stood. More things scurried around us. We stood with our backs to each other like the four final cavalrymen at Little Bighorn. The noise abruptly ended.

In the depths of the old house someone screamed.

"Kara?" Chelsea guessed.

Ian Tremblin snatched the lantern. Like the mirror at the end of the hallway, his eyes reflected the flame dancing atop the remaining candle. "I think it's time we looked for our missing comrades."

Demarius plucked the candle from the candelabrum and handed it to the writer.

I don't know how long we explored, but it felt like hours. Our eyesight had grown accustomed to candlelight, so even in the gloom we could make out much of Daemon Hall. We started on the third floor, which was mainly bedroom suites.

Tremblin paused in the hallway. "The Daemon family had their personal rooms in this part of the house," he said, and opened a door. "This is where the bodies of the Daemon twins were discovered. They lay in bed looking as peaceful as sleeping angels. The official report said they were smothered with a pillow, but that wouldn't jibe with their relaxed, serene expressions. It's just one of the many mysteries of the house."

We continued. The lantern provided a small pool of light that illuminated the gloomy hall. The upper half of the walls were painted in some dark hue, the lower half had vertical slats of dark wood, similar to the hardwood floor. A narrow carpet runner ran down the center of the hallway.

"Like her brothers, Cornelia Daemon was found in her room," Ian Tremblin said, opening another door. "And like her brothers, she was in bed, at peace, dead."

"Why?" Chelsea whispered. "I mean, why would a father do something like that to his own family?"

The author quietly closed the door to Cornelia's room and continued. "Rudolph Daemon was always considered an exemplary family man, a brilliant businessman, and something of a philanthropist. All that changed shortly after he moved his family into Daemon Hall. As I see it, there are two possible scenarios. One: he went insane, something totally independent of the mansion. Two: there really is an evil influence in Daemon Hall and it twisted the man."

"Like Stephen King's *The Shining*," Chelsea said.

"Just like it," Demarius muttered.

Ian Tremblin nodded. "And considering what we have seen tonight, I fear that option is the correct one."

"You underestimated the house," I said.

"Totally my fault," the writer replied. "I had no idea that Daemon Hall would turn out to be as malevolent and—and—as insatiable as it is."

Chelsea marched ahead. "Regret won't do us any good. We need to find Kara and Chris, and then figure out how to get out."

She stopped; the hallway ended at an arched doorway set in a rounded stone wall. The large door was made from hefty planks of wood held together by black metal bands. A thick metal hoop hung where there should have been a doorknob.

Ian Tremblin held the lantern up to the door. "You can see by the architecture that Rudolph Daemon was fond of castles. He made it even more so for his own personal study."

He pulled on the metal ring and the heavy door opened. We trailed him into the room. It was in one of the towers built into the corners of the mansion and the room was round. The walls were bare stone except where two large tapestries hung. A kidney-shaped mahogany desk sat in the middle of the room. Two large arched windows looked out over the grounds. I went to one of the windows and gazed down. Rudolph Daemon's office was at least fifty feet aboveground.

Turning to the others, I saw them all looking straight up. "What?"

Ian Tremblin held the lantern high. "We're trying to see the ceiling of the room. Unfortunately, it's too high up for this single candle." He lowered the lantern. "The ceiling is domed, and about twenty-five feet over our heads. Just under the dome is where two beams cross. That was where Rudolph was found the morning after he killed his family. He had tied a rope to those beams and hanged himself."

"At least they knew how he died, unlike his kids," Chelsea said.

"Ah, but there is a mystery concerning Rudolph's death as well. A ladder was not found in the room. How was it then that he climbed up to the ceiling to commit suicide?"

As if hoping the answers could be seen above, Ian Tremblin held the lantern up again. I stared upward, and for a brief moment thought I saw the bottoms of two feet swaying in the shadows.

"Can we get out of here?" I said a bit too loudly.

"Yeah, I second that." Demarius nodded.

After Tremblin shut the door, Chelsea asked, "What about Mrs. Daemon, what happened to her?"

Ian Tremblin retraced our steps a short distance, stopping before an oak door. He pushed it open, and we followed him inside. "The master suite," he said. The room was huge. Tremblin led us through the middle; nearby furnishings were merely dark shapes in the candle glow. He opened another door and thrust the lantern inside. Immediately, like a visual echo, our light was joined by countless others.

"What's that?" Demarius asked.

"Come inside."

We followed the writer into an oddly shaped room. Two doors were open, the one we'd entered, and another one halfway round the room. The walls were covered with floor-to-ceiling mirrors.

"Rudolph Daemon liked castles," Ian Tremblin said. "His wife was fond of mirrors, or to be more exact, what she saw in mirrors. This was part of her dressing room."

It was incredible. Each mirror reflected the candlelight and then reflected a reflection and a reflection of a reflection of a reflection. It was eternity encased in one creepy room. And like the candle, we were reflected endlessly in a sea of glass.

"Man," Demarius said, which pretty much summed up how I felt about it.

"This room is ten-sided, a decagon. Each wall has a mirror, even on the backs of the doors, so make sure you don't close them." He reached out and touched the one that opened to the master suite. "It's easy to get confused and you'll have a hard time finding your way out."

"I can understand a full-length mirror, or even a three-sided mirror. But why all this?" Chelsea asked.

"Rudolph's wife, Narcissa, was well named. She spent hours each day trying on various wardrobes and admiring her infinite reflections. She was considered a self-centered woman before their move to Daemon Hall. It was after they had lived here for a short while that her self-love became an obsession. According to those who knew her, she ignored her children, her husband, her friends, and concentrated solely on her true love: herself."

"How did Rudolph kill her?" I asked, not sure I wanted to know.

"We don't know. Her body was never found."

"Damn," Demarius said, spinning in the ten-sided room, watching his myriad of reflections do the same.

"Would you like to hear one of the legends?" Ian Tremblin asked, then continued, not waiting for an answer. "Shortly after the crimes, when curiosity seekers still had the courage to come to Daemon Hall, stories began to circulate about this room. Narcissa, some people claimed, could be seen in the mirrors.

Not her reflection, mind you, but Narcissa herself—inside the mirrors."

"I'm getting dizzy in here," Chelsea said.

Ian Tremblin pointed to the other open door and handed Chelsea the lantern. "Go through there. That's where Narcissa's closets are. You'll find several portraits of her hanging on the walls."

We started for the closets, but Ian Tremblin remained.

"Aren't you coming?" I asked.

"No. I want to see if Narcissa will show herself to me."

I followed Chelsea and Demarius down a short hallway into a changing room. Except for a small settee and three portraits, the room was empty. Each wall, including the one that opened onto the small hallway, had a door in it.

"Mr. Tremblin," Demarius called, "where do the doors lead?"

The author wasn't that far from us, yet it sounded as if his voice came from a greater distance. "Each door opens to a closet for each season: the spring wardrobes, the autumn wardrobes, the summer and the winter wardrobes."

"That's why I like black," Chelsea said. "Goes with any season. Hey, come check out Narcissa's pictures." Chelsea lifted the lantern to three paintings of Mrs. Daemon. The first was a close-up of her face, the next detailed her full body, and a third was a landscape of the surrounding grounds with Narcissa standing front and center.

"Whoa, she's gorgeous," Demarius said.

Narcissa was a contrast of natural color: sky-blue eyes, rose-petal cheeks, cherry lips, and ivory skin. A mane of dark chestnut hair flowed past her shoulders.

"Yeah," I agreed.

"But look at her eyes." Chelsea tapped the portrait of Narcissa's face. "The lights are on, but nobody's home. Let's check out her clothes."

Chelsea stepped toward the first door, and Demarius called out, "Hey, Mr. Tremblin, can we go through the stuff in the closets?"

Chelsea reached for the knob. Tremblin gave no reply.

"Mr. Tremblin?" Chelsea called out loudly, hand inches from the door.

We heard a click. Chelsea pulled back her hand, and all three of us stared in disbelief as the knob on the closet door twisted by itself. We all backed up a step. The knob stopped turning, and a black crack appeared as the door opened outward.

Demarius spoke, voice breaking, "You know, whenever you guys want to run, just let me know."

"Wait," Chelsea whispered.

Mesmerized, we watched the door open fully. A tall, lanky figure took a step toward us, stopping just inside the closet.

"Mr. Tremblin," Demarius said with shaky relief. "Jeez, you scared us."

"Is that a secret passage or something?" Chelsea asked.

Ian Tremblin didn't answer. Instead he stood rigidly, his attention fixed over our heads. "Is that a secret passage or something?" he said in a perfect impersonation of Chelsea.

We stared dumbly at him. Just as I struggled to talk, the door slammed shut. We jumped, and the door in the next wall opened. Ian Tremblin—another Ian Tremblin—stepped forward so that we could see him in the dim lantern-light. As before, he stood rigid, but this time his head moved side to side as if he were looking for us. But it was questionable that this Ian Tremblin could see; his eyes were completely white.

"Are you okay, Mr. Tremblin?" Demarius asked.

The writer's unseeing gaze stopped in the direction of Demarius. "Are you okay, Mr. Tremblin?" It was Demarius's voice coming from Ian Tremblin's mouth.

That door slammed, and the next flew open to reveal another Ian Tremblin. His lifeless white eyes were in constant motion, stretching, widening, and elongating.

"Let's get the hell out of here," I said in a rush.

"Let's get the hell out of here," the doppelganger repeated in my voice. The door boomed shut.

What I feared most happened next. The final door in the changing room opened, and like obedient children, we stood there and watched as the fourth Ian Tremblin stepped into our light. Instead of eyes, two arched windows—windows exactly like those in Rudolph Daemon's study—gaped from behind his

spectacles. There was a dim light behind those windows, and the silhouette of a tiny figure swinging back and forth.

His mouth opened, and he howled as if in pain.

The door banged shut and we ran. When we entered the mirrored room, the hall door shut behind us—the other door was already closed. We turned this way and that, spun round and round, and ended up totally disoriented.

"Which mirror is the door out of here?" Demarius asked, breathless. His numerous reflections silently mouthed along.

"What happened to Mr. Tremblin?" Chelsea cast quick glances around the room, which caused her mirror images to look in every imaginable direction.

Then I saw it, though I wasn't sure what it was. We were reflected on all ten walls, and those reflections cast their own, and so on. It seemed like we were a crowd, a rabble, a terrified mob. Yet in one mirror, there was a growing figure over our image. I pointed to it, unable to speak. The image grew until we could see it was a person, lanky and uncoordinated, running for all he was worth toward us. Ian Tremblin. Demarius gasped like he'd been belly-punched and sank to his knees.

"Mr.—" Chelsea started to say, but the rest of his name died on her lips.

Legs furiously pumping, he could obviously see us. His mouth worked feverishly, as if he were yelling at us, yet we couldn't hear him. When he finally got close, he ran headlong into the other side of the mirror like it was a solid wall. He flew back, legs over his head, and landed hard on his back. After a stunned moment, he climbed to his feet and carefully approached the mirror. Holding his hands before him, he stepped cautiously forward until he touched the back side of the glass. Demarius, Chelsea, and I still cast incalculable reflections, yet there was only one Ian Tremblin. He ran his hands up and down the mirror, his fearful face crumbled into terrified panic. He clenched his fists and began to hit the mirror, trying to break through. As hard as his punches were, we still heard no sound.

Chelsea stepped forward and placed a hand on the mirror. Ian Tremblin stopped his assault on the glass and looked at her with frightened resignation. Slowly he lifted a hand and placed it next to hers on the opposite side of the looking glass.

"Oh, Mr. Tremblin," Chelsea grieved.

Ian Tremblin turned as if he heard something. He stared back at us, panic on his face anew. He ran. Whatever pursued him must have been frightening, yet it was invisible to us. He ran in circles around the decagon room, going farther out with each lap until he finally faded among our limitless reflections.

Demarius shot to his feet and ran to the mirrors. He ran his fingers up the crease separating two angles of the room. Chelsea and I saw what he was doing and did the same.

I found the door latch. "Here!" I shouted. "Here it is!"

I pulled the door open, and we ran from the room through the master suite. In the hallway we continued running. Chelsea led the way, holding the lantern high, its meager light bouncing in our panicked flight. We turned a corner, and then another before we stopped abruptly, our way blocked by Ian Tremblin.

"There you are," his voice rumbled. "I wondered where you had gotten off to." He reached out and snatched the lantern from Chelsea's fingers. "I think we've seen enough of the third floor, don't you?"

We followed the writer down to the second floor in stunned silence. Questions about what had happened, what we had seen, flooded my mind, yet I couldn't seem to form the words to ask them.

Finally, Chelsea grabbed the writer by his shoulder and spun him around. "Wait a minute, Mr. Tremblin. What happened to you?"

"Happened to me? What do you mean?" Though he wasn't smiling, there was humor in his voice. His black eyes no longer sparkled in the candle glow. Instead they seemed to absorb the light and trap it inside, revealing only a flat, lusterless gaze.

"We left you in the mirrored room. What happened there?" Demarius asked.

"Nothing. I went for a stroll. Why? Did something happen?"

"Yeah," Demarius said. "We saw—"

"We thought we saw something weird," I interrupted. Something about the writer made me uncomfortable. I looked carefully at both Chelsea and Demarius and tried to communicate with my eyes. "Probably our imaginations."

They looked at me, puzzled, but didn't say any more about it.

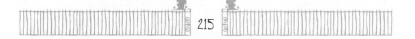

"Probably," the writer agreed, and we began our search again.

After the second floor, we skipped the first to look in the basement for Kara and Chris. The basement was a maze of brick-walled corridors and low-ceilinged rooms. Just as Demarius commented on how the basement would be the perfect setting for Poe's "Cask of Amontillado," we discovered the wine cellar. Row upon row of dusty bottles sat inclined in wooden racks.

"I don't suppose any of you brought a corkscrew?" Ian Tremblin asked, literally licking his lips.

"Try me in five years when I'm twenty-one," Demarius answered.

"A shame. I like wine. Not white, but red—very, very red." He grinned.

In one dank room we noticed a hatch in the floor. I pulled it up by a large metal ring. Steep wooden steps descended into darkness.

"Whoa, man! Stinks like a sewer down there." Demarius waved a hand in front of his face.

"Anyone care to look?" Ian Tremblin asked all of us, though he held the lantern out to me.

I took it.

"Be careful," Chelsea said from behind her hand.

"I'm not going all the way." I counted seven steps down and stopped, my head just below the trapdoor. I held the lantern low and saw there were a dozen more steps to the subbasement floor.

I heard running water. A narrow creek ran from my right into the gloom to my left.

"What is it? What do you see?" Demarius asked.

"I think you're right," I called up. "It's some kind of old sewer."

An object floated into view. I took a couple more steps down for a better look. In the murkiness it resembled a half-sunken beach ball revolving in a lazy circle. When it drifted by my perch, it spun, and I saw that it was Chris. His head was all that was visible, the nose, eyes, and forehead bobbing above the water. Open eyes rolled back, revealing only whites. The head carouseled languidly downstream until it passed out of the lantern light.

Like a breath, I heard Chris's voice. *"Come on in, Wade. The water's fine."*

I scrambled up the steps, dropped the lantern, and slammed the hatch shut.

"What happened?" Chelsea asked, placing her hand on my shoulder.

I covered my face. My body trembled.

"What did you see?" Demarius asked.

"Nothing," I mumbled from behind my hands. I could never talk about this. If I tried, I'd finally go totally, absolutely, pedal-to-the-metal crazy.

"Don't you want to tell us what you saw?" Ian Tremblin said.

I dropped my hands and shouted, "I didn't see a damn thing!"

A slight smile on his face, Tremblin said, "Wade, calm down. *Try and keep your head above water.*"

I gasped.

He chuckled as he picked up the lantern. "Let's continue."

From the basement, the writer led us to a monstrous room on the first floor. Stars twinkled through a large gap in the ceiling.

"The swimming pool," the author said. He pointed up. "The retractable roof could be opened and closed. Looks like it got jammed slightly open."

We approached the not-quite-Olympic-sized pool. Cracks lined the concrete sides. It was empty except for a few feet of stagnant black water in the deep end. A skeletal wooden frame that once held a high dive stood barren. Next to it, the low diving board still perched out over the slimy, deep-end water.

"Wow! What a pool!" Demarius exclaimed.

"Yeah, it's great," Chelsea said, "if you like your pool scummy and falling to pieces."

"Look how clear and blue the water is," Demarius said.

"Clear and blue? Only if you're used to swimming at sewage treatment plants." I thought Demarius was kidding. It would've been like him to try and bring some levity to our situation.

Moving as if in a daze, Demarius stripped off his shirt and kicked off his shoes and socks. He stepped onto the diving board. "Refreshing. It'll be so refreshing and cool to take a swim."

"Cut it out, Demarius. We're here to look for Kara," Chelsea said, and I detected a note of concern in her voice.

Demarius, without hesitation, walked to the very end of the diving board.

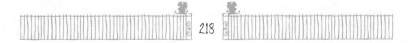

"Oh my God," Chelsea yelled.

"Hey! Demarius! What are you doing?" I shouted.

I turned briefly and caught a quick glimpse of Ian Tremblin watching with a small grin.

Demarius jumped up and down several times, testing the bounce of the board. My heart stopped as I thought what would happen to him if he fell the fifteen or so feet into the nearly empty pool.

"Demarius, listen to me," I said. "Don't do—"

"Go swimming. Go swimming," Demarius intoned, "so relaxing. Swimming is so relaxing. Everything will be fine once I dive in."

"Hey, dumb ass!" Chelsea screamed as loud as she could, and it snapped the spell Demarius had been under.

He blinked several times and looked around. When he glanced down and saw the empty pool below him, he lost his balance and nearly fell. "What the—? I was—there was a pool here a second ago, a real pool, full of water, clear water, and—"

"Demarius," Chelsea said in a low, calm voice, "get off that diving board."

Before he got off, we heard a plaintive call from the hallway: "Please, why won't you let me leave?"

"Kara!" Chelsea yelled.

"Kara! Hey, Kara!" I shouted, and ran for the entrance, Chelsea at my heels.

But the hallway was empty.

"Kara, Kara, where are you?" Chelsea and I shouted.

There was no reply.

The writer stood unmoving by the pool, and I took advantage of the short distance between him and us. "Chelsea," I whispered, "do you notice anything strange about Tremblin since the mirrors—"

"Hey!" Demarius cried.

The writer stared at him perched on the diving board. A cracking sound resonated. The diving board split in half, and Demarius fell from view.

We rushed to the pool.

"The wood was rotted. He fell in," Ian Tremblin stated in the same voice he would have used to say, *A lovely day we're having.*

"I didn't hear a splash!" Chelsea said behind me.

I ran to the shallow end of the pool, jumped down, and slogged into the deep-end water. Chelsea grabbed the lantern from Tremblin, knelt, and held it so that I could see as I made my way through the waist-deep muck. I splashed around in that nasty black water, feeling for Demarius from one side of the pool to the next, then looked up.

"He's not in here."

We searched the entire swimming area, including the changing rooms and steam bath. Worried that I'd somehow missed Demarius, I forced myself back into that soupy water but found nothing. We returned to the study, stopping briefly at a bedroom so that I could pull a mildewed blanket from a bed and wrap it around my wet body.

Ian Tremblin transferred the candle from the lantern to the candelabrum. *"Three little finalists made up this hearty crew— one was forced to walk the plank and then there were two."*

"What is wrong with you?" Chelsea demanded.

The writer didn't answer but continued his poem. *"Two little finalists, one went on the run—screamed and tripped and broke a neck and then there was one."*

I finished dazedly. *"The last little finalist almost had it won— that finalist went insane and then there were none."*

Chelsea pushed up from her seat and paced before the candelabrum. "That only leaves Wade and me. Gee, Wade, which do you prefer? The broken neck or insanity?"

I shivered, knowing which fate awaited me.

"Chelsea. Putting up a brave front with sarcasm. How like you." The writer sneered in the candlelight.

"Is any of this real?" Chelsea asked.

"Or are we simply a story within a story?" Tremblin answered with a question.

"No! I'm real!" she shouted. "I'm a teenager, I go to Westview High, and I like to write. I write well enough that I became a finalist in your stupid contest. And you know what? You're not scaring me off. I'm sticking with it until the end! I'm going to win!" She flung herself into the nearest chair.

"Chelsea, the contest isn't important anymore," I pleaded.

Ian Tremblin spoke in a low rumble. "Oh, but you're wrong. Tonight, the contest is the most important thing in your lives."

I felt strange, like I was bordering on an attack. I looked around the room. In the dim glow of that last candle, the stuffed heads on the wall looked more like monsters than animals. The fireplace seemed like a cave where something squishy, evil, and hungry lay in wait. The metal framework of the candelabrum resembled a tangle of spiderwebs.

"We are down to the secret candle," Ian Tremblin said, eyes hidden in shadow.

Chelsea looked at him suspiciously.

"Secret candle?" I asked.

"One candle provides enough light for us to see, but also allows enough darkness so that we should feel safe in unloading a burden, sharing a secret."

"Sounds like a slumber party," Chelsea said. "Truth or Dare."

"Oh, it'll be much deeper than that. Look at the glow cast by this one candle. We can just see each other, but the cold darkness that surrounds our candle-fed existence could very well signify nothingness. It's as though we are the last three people left in the world. We should feel safe to reach into our souls and bare secrets that fuel great shame. I, for one, know I need to relieve a terrible burden."

I sat heavily in a chair. "Fine, but I don't have any secrets."

"That is not true, Wade," the writer said. "Tonight I make the rules. Call me a nosy, manipulative power monger if you want, but to win you will have to take me into your confidence.

We all have something we can divulge by the glow of the secret candle."

"What is your secret, Mr. Tremblin?" Chelsea asked.

"Everything in its own time, Chelsea. Perhaps you have the courage to begin."

She nodded once as if taking a dare. Her strands of red hair glowed like a hot flame. Shadows combined with her black eye liner to give her face a skull-like cast. "I have a secret." She looked down at her lap and whispered, "The image is always in my mind.

"I said that I don't like Maplewood because it changes people. I didn't mean me. I meant my father. Mr. Donald 'Call Me Don' Flynt, family man and businessman. It happened at the start of school last year, right after we moved from Florida. Dad came a couple of months before Mom and me. He had to start his new job, and Mom had to work a few more weeks at her old job. I wanted to finish the school year with my friends. Mom and I used to feel sorry for Dad all by himself in Maplewood. See, we didn't know he'd found someone to play with.

"Things seemed fine after Mom and I arrived. One day after school I decided I'd go downtown to Dad's office and catch a ride home with him. No big reason. We were close." Her voice remained steady, but a tear fell and landed on her hand. "He has this secretary, Donna, and she's built like a lingerie model. Her face isn't very pretty, but I guess most guys can't get their gaze up

past her chest. Donna wasn't at her desk, so I went to Dad's office and opened the door. They didn't see me, but I saw them. I saw Dad and Donna—together. I shut the door and left.

"Dad thinks the reason I won't give him the time of day is because of adolescence. I want to tell him the real reason—I want him to see that he's the one who stole our relationship, but I can't. I feel guilty for not telling Mom. I'm so frustrated. All I want is to be a normal daughter in a normal family." She looked up. Tears mingled with her makeup, leaving black tracks down her cheeks. "But he took that from me."

"Sins of the father have damned many a family," Ian Tremblin said softly.

"It's not your fault, Chelsea." I felt bad for her. "You shouldn't feel guilty."

Ian Tremblin leaned into the candle glow. His eyes were still dull and muted. "If you were to speak with your father about what you saw, Chelsea, would you forgive him or condemn him?"

She didn't answer but stared angrily at the writer.

"Yes," Ian Tremblin growled, "condemnation is good. But take heart. You have been an inspiration. You have shown us how to confide in one another by the light of the secret candle. Are you ready, Wade?"

I didn't say a thing. The candle flame jumped and flickered, causing shadows to waltz around Tremblin. Chelsea hugged herself. The candle sputtered and flared. The flame doubled

and then tripled in size. A scream ripped through the house. Footsteps thumped as someone ran past the open double doors of the study and down the hall.

"Kara!" Chelsea gasped and rushed to the doors.

Ian Tremblin gave her a chilling smile. "Seriously, Chelsea, there is nothing we can do for her until I—until the house chooses to give up its grasp."

Chelsea dashed through the doors and turned after the retreating footsteps. I tried to follow, but the doors swung shut. The clunk of engaging locks echoed in the study. I worked at the doors in vain.

I shouted at the writer. "What's happening?"

Ian Tremblin held a hand to his chest. "I'm waiting for your shame. The house won't let you leave this room until you honor us at the secret candle."

I shook my head.

"You have to share your secret with me—with the house."

Someone ran up the hallway. The doorknobs twisted and the doors rattled.

"Wade! I need help!" Chelsea shouted from the other side.

I flew at the doors, pushing and pulling. "I can't! The doors won't open!"

There was a scream from the front of the house, and Chelsea ran off.

"You can be just as brave as her," Ian Tremblin said. "All you

have to do is tell your secret. That takes even more courage than running around Daemon Hall in the dark."

"I can't," I whispered.

"You can. And when you do, your shame will be cast off, and you shall be set free."

I looked from Ian Tremblin to the closed doors and back again.

Chelsea called from deep in the house, "Wade, help me!"

I folded into the chair nearest the lone candle and wrapped both arms around my head.

Ian Tremblin cleared his throat and waited a beat. "Wade, your secret, please."

I lifted my head to glance at the writer. "My balance is . . . faltering."

"Your balance?"

"I think—sometimes I think—I'm going crazy."

"My goodness." The writer watched me with hungry expectation.

"I have these fears. I get scared, terrified, but not at anything in particular. Sometimes, from out of nowhere, a wave of fear hits me. That's what it's like, a wave washing over me. I can hardly move, I can't talk, I can barely breathe. It feels like my heart is going to burst. I lose track of time. I don't know where I am or what I'm doing. If there's a dark, sheltered spot nearby, I'll go there to hide till it ends, though I'm always afraid that it never will."

"Have you spoken with anyone about this?"

"No. Never."

"How long has madness been knocking at your door?" An undercurrent of glee colored his question.

"A year, maybe a year and a half. I used to only get attacks once in a while, but lately I've been getting more, a bunch more."

"Considering your frail mental condition, don't you find it strange that you entered a contest that would put you in a haunted house for a night?"

"That's why tonight is so important. Whether I win or not doesn't matter, but if I can survive this place, then maybe nothing else can frighten me."

"It's not whether you win or lose, it's whether you keep your sanity. Is that it?"

"I'm hoping that if I outlast whatever tonight has in store for me, I won't have any more attacks. I won't go crazy."

"They say it's dangerous to prescribe your own therapy, Wade. On the other hand, I can't imagine anything topping tonight on the fear meter. My guess is that it will either be very good for you—or you'll lose it altogether."

"Yeah," I agreed. "That's my secret."

A snap as loud as a pistol shot caused me to jump. The doors unlocked and swung open.

Ian Tremblin picked up the remaining candle, now burnt low, placed it in his lantern, and handed it to me. "Go find your fellow finalist and return. You know that no one will be allowed to leave until the tenth story is told."

I stepped through the door into the hallway, and Ian Tremblin called my name. He was still seated, and since I held the lantern, I couldn't see his features. He was merely a silhouette wrapped in shadows.

"What?"

"I haven't shared my secret."

"Look, we don't have time—"

Ian Tremblin stood. I stared numbly as he shuffled close enough for me to see him. As in the final closet, the windows of Daemon Hall were where his eyes should have been. In place of his mouth was a miniature version of the door leading into this hellish home. He reached up and twisted the tiny doorknob and pulled the door open, revealing a black maw. Words, like gusts of wind, blew from the doorway.

"I AM DAEMON HALL."

I screamed and fled in the direction Chelsea had run, through dark halls and narrow corridors, pursued by echoing laughter. I ran, not to help Chelsea but because I was terrified of being alone with what had once been Ian Tremblin. I shouted Chelsea's name. She didn't answer, so I shouted again and again. I yelled her name once more, and as the echo died, I saw her lying at the bottom of the staircase. I hurried down the stairs two at a time, the rhythm of my feet slapping the marble like a metronome, until I knelt by her, holding the lantern near her face.

"No—no—nooo . . ."

Her expression was slack, and her head rested at an odd angle. Not wanting to, I touched her neck. She was cold, and I felt bone press against skin. I picked up her wrist; there was no pulse.

"Help me! Someone help, please. Chelsea is hurt! She's hurt bad," I yelled. "I think she may be—I think Chelsea is—" I stopped as the rusty hinges of the distant door began singing.

The front door opened. Compared to the darkness inside Daemon Hall, the night outside seemed as light as day. I felt like Peter in Kara's poem: on the inside looking out. But now I had a chance to escape. I thought about my plan to survive Daemon Hall and cure my unnamed affliction. How stupid. I'd leave. I'd find Ian Tremblin's driver at the front gate, call the police, and put an end to whatever was happening.

I took a shambling step toward the door and stopped, willing it to stay open. I took three more steps, my eyes never wavering from my goal, afraid that if I glanced away the door would close. Step by step, I picked up speed and almost made it, but the house was teasing me. The door boomed shut, sealing me inside.

Five little finalists waiting by the door—Chris vanished down a hole and then there were four.

I spun.

Four little finalists plain for all to see—Kara was dragged into the night and then there were three.

Was it just in my head?

Three little finalists made up this hearty crew—Demarius walked the plank and then there were two.

"Mr. Tremblin! Is that you?"

Two little finalists, one went on the run—Chelsea tripped and broke her neck and then there was one.

"WHO'S SAYING THAT?" I yelled.

The last little finalist almost had it won—sadly, Wade went insane—

I felt it. Another attack—episode—bout of insanity coming on.

Sadly, Wade went insane—

My heartbeat doubled and doubled again.

Sadly, Wade went insane—

I tried to focus on the lantern by Chelsea's body. Dizziness hit me, and the lantern rose and fell as if it floated on stormy seas. I closed my eyes.

Sadly, Wade went insane—

The wave I'd described to Mr. Tremblin, the wave of fear, broke over me.

Sadly, Wade went insane—

"Open your eyes, Wade." The voice came from in front of me.

Sadly, Wade went insane—

"Everything is fine—at least for the moment." It was Ian Tremblin.

Sadly, Wade went insane—

"Open your eyes."

I did and would have collapsed had there not been a chair to grab. I was no longer in the entry hall but had somehow returned

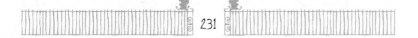

to the upstairs study. I sat quickly, worried that dizziness would drop me to the floor. The lantern, empty, sat by the candelabrum upon which one low-burnt candle radiated its pathetic glow.

Ian Tremblin patted my knee reassuringly. I stared at him, wondering if he or the malignant essence of Daemon Hall watched me through those cold black eyes.

He leaned back and spoke. "We've all heard of ghost towns. Those deserted Old West towns. Did you know there are such things as ghost cities? They are rare, but now and then throughout history a ghost city will evolve. A place where hundreds of thousands or even millions of residents will just leave. Sometimes there's an explanation. Maybe the city comes under military siege, perhaps a major water supply dries up, or disease chases off the inhabitants. Sometimes there is no logical explanation. Sometimes the explanations are things we would rather not know."

Don't Go into the Shadows

We see two figures strolling up the middle of a city street. There are cars, though they're not moving. Most are parked haphazardly, as if the drivers stopped, got out, and walked away. We look for other people, other signs of life, but it's just these two. As they get closer, we see one of them is a pleasant-looking typical teenager. It's easy to tell he just arrived. Another runaway who came looking for adventure. The other, however, has all kinds of things strapped to his body and hanging from his belt.

The normal-looking one says, "The shadows?"

"Dude, that's the important thing. Don't go into the shadows."

"You mean at night? 'Cause they sleep during the day, right?" Sean asked. With his golf shirt and nearly new jeans, he was a complete contrast to Kid.

"You newbies are something else," Kid said in disgust. "I been in this city all my life. The change started when I was only nine years old. I'm still alive because I know what the hell I'm talking about. Now pay attention! Shadows are always dangerous, day or night. Night's more dangerous 'cause there's more darkness."

Kid's hair was black and long. His clothes were tattered and dirty, from his sleeveless T-shirt and well-worn black leather vest to his khaki pants, cut off just below the knee. Worn-out moccasins protected his feet. A quiver from a bow and arrow set had been strapped diagonally across his back and held a metal baseball bat.

Across his waist hung a carpenter's belt with a variety of flashlights dangling from leather loops. Rounding out his flashlit wardrobe were the extra batteries he carried in bandoliers he'd fashioned from two leather belts.

"I always heard that Shadow Eaters didn't come out till night," Sean said.

"That's why most of you newbies don't last but a day or two."

They continued in silence until Sean asked, "If one of your generators still runs, why are we going to get another one?"

"The key to makin' it in the city is having what you need and then having backups. My main generator blew last night. Shadow Eaters would've had a hell of a feast if I didn't have that backup. So now we gotta get a replacement generator for the one that crapped out. Remember that. Backups for every damn thing."

They walked several miles from Kid's home, a fortified apartment on the twelfth floor of a skyscraper. Kid had strengthened the doors and walls, installed surveillance cameras, and wired his apartment so that it was powered by generators. He'd scavenged so much dried and canned food over the years that it nearly filled a small bedroom. Once inside, he bragged he could withstand a Shadow Eater siege for weeks, maybe even months. That was why he called his home the Twelfth-Floor Blockade. Sean had been staying with him ever since Kid found him wandering the streets a few days earlier. They turned onto a street that had once featured upscale shopping. Continuing for two more blocks, Kid stopped before a store. The sign read GRENDEL'S.

Sean said, "I used to watch the Grendel's Christmas Parade on television before—you know."

"I was there," Kid stated. "My folks brought me to see it every year."

"What happened to your parents?"

"What do you think?"

Sean followed Kid through a shattered plate-glass window and stepped carefully over glass shards into the biggest store he'd ever seen. "This place is huge."

"Grendel's has got five floors and a sublevel. Dude, they had everything: clothes, toys, huntin' gear, you name it. Now there ain't much of nothin' left—at least aboveground."

"But there are generators?"

"Oh, yeah. Down there." Kid pointed at the floor. "In the basement, there's still pretty much everything."

"The basement!" Sean said. "But aren't there—you know?"

"Shadow Eaters down there? Yeah, the place is crawling with them." Kid grinned. "That's why nobody bothers with what's down there. But don't worry, I have it fixed. Those numb-munchers ain't gonna get us."

"I'm not going down there, Kid! You crazy? The closest I've ever been to a Shadow Eater is a block away, and I still ran like hell."

"You been a lot closer, you just didn't know it. They're everywhere it's dark, like cockroaches." Kid put a hand on Sean's shoulder. "Look, I need help to get a generator. We both need it to survive. I ain't gonna lie and say it's safe. I guaran-damn-tee that this'll be the closest you'll come to Shadow Eaters and live. But live we will, dude. Trust me."

"I hope you know what you're doing."

"Here, take this." Kid unhooked a squat utility flashlight from his tool belt and passed it to Sean. He took out a long black flashlight for himself.

They went deeper into Grendel's. The light waned steadily as they moved from the windows. Kid passed an elevator and stopped at the top of an unmoving escalator. Racks of merchandise stood in the murky light that spilled into the basement. They heard the subtle sound of movement below.

"Turn on your light," Kid said.

Sean followed Kid down the escalator, moving his light around. Once on the basement floor, scuttling figures emerged from the dark; the Shadow Eaters were coming. In brief glimpses Sean saw blank, slack-jawed faces. Gelatinous saliva coated their chins. Their pale skin peeled in dry flakes. It looked like their lips, nostrils, and the skin around their eyes had been dusted with charcoal. Their clothes were little more than rags. Some sported wounds, caused both before and after death.

"Are you sure this is okay?" Sean whispered, flashing on two numb-munchers. Both made throaty noises and shambled back into darkness.

Kid unclipped another flashlight and waved both horizontally. "I ain't never seen 'em this thick." Kid led them across the floor. "But it's cool. We have our lights."

"These are new batteries, right?" Sean's voice shook.

Kid replaced one flashlight on his belt and held out the other. "They're new, and we're here. Take my flashlight and keep 'em away."

A plastic plaque with the words EMPLOYEES ONLY was mounted on a door. A large padlock on a hinged clasp secured it. Kid shoved a key in the lock and clicked it open. They went in and Kid snapped the lock shut on another clasp inside the door.

"Breathe easy, dude," Kid said.

Sean shone his light around the room. They were in a large storage closet. In the center stood a piece of machinery.

"A generator?" Sean guessed.

"Yeah. Bigger than the one we're picking up." Kid checked the levels of gas and oil. "Me and a couple of friends, Joseph and Discman, hooked it up. It was Discman's idea."

"Discman?"

" 'Cause he wore CDs on a chain around his neck. We came in one day loaded with battery-powered lamps to keep the Shadow Eaters away. We hooked up this generator to the lighting in the basement. We each got a key to the lock so that any time we needed something, we could come on down." Kid took back his flashlight and pointed it to illuminate the end of the generator, where black cables snaked out and up into the drop ceiling. "There's lotsa good stuff down here that the others don't take 'cause of the Shadow Eaters. All we had to do was hook up the generator. Seemed easy enough."

"Creepy!" Sean glanced nervously at the door. They could hear feet shuffling on the other side.

Kid nodded. "We ran cables through the drop ceiling and hooked 'em to the lights from above. We were about done when Joseph fell through the ceiling. The Shadow Eaters were on him like white on rice, lice on mice, and cold on ice. We tried to help, but there were too many."

"That sucks."

"It gets worse." Kid looked at Sean. "A Shadow Eater bit Discman, took a chunk outta his arm when we were trying to save Joseph. That numb-muncher's spit was poisonin' him by the time I got him back to the Twelfth-Floor Blockade. He lasted three days."

"Man," Sean muttered.

"It wasn't pretty. Ol' Disc tried to fight the poisons, but it got him. I put him outside the blockade door. He reanimated, and I ain't never seen him again." Kid pulled a cord, and the generator fired up.

"Here's the fun part." He flipped a lever. For a brief second the generator's hum dropped a notch, then rose to its original pitch as the lights flared on.

"Ta-dah! Not only lights in here, but all over the basement. Listen."

Muted screams began on the other side of the door. Crashes joined the guttural moans as Shadow Eaters knocked over displays in their quest for a dark recess.

Kid laughed, his ear at the door. "Funny as hell. But remember that they're hungry all the time, even on the run. So let's give 'em a few minutes to get into their hidey-holes."

Kid saw the unease on Sean's face. "Hey, we'll be okay with the lights on. These things run on instinct. Instinct number one is to get out of light. Instinct number two is to eat people. Long as we got lights, instinct number one overrides instinct number two."

After several minutes the sounds died down. Kid clipped the flashlights they'd used on his belt and opened the door. He relocked the door after Sean. They went through sporting goods and automotive before arriving in the lawn and hardware department. They walked past mowers and power trimmers, stopping at a stack of large boxes.

"Here. We'll run it up to the street." They each picked up an end of a heavy box. Kid smiled. "Like havin' our own private store." Kid's grin vanished. Everything disappeared. All the lights in the basement went out.

"Kid!"

"Uh-oh."

"Kid! What do we do?"

"We get the hell out of here," Kid said, and dropped his side of the box. The other side tumbled from Sean's grasp. Light flared. Kid had his flashlight in hand and quickly passed the utility flashlight to Sean. "Let's go." They ran, motivated by the sound of Shadow Eaters emerging from their dark holes.

"Shine 'em with your light!" Kid ordered.

Sean desperately swept the flashlight back and forth. Kid yelled as a shadowy figure grabbed at him from behind. His flashlight was knocked from his grasp and skittered down an aisle beside stacked bags of topsoil. Sean swung his flashlight as Kid pulled the baseball bat from across his back and whacked the head of an attacking Shadow Eater.

"Sweep 'em with the light!" Kid shouted, but Sean was mesmerized by the sight of the Shadow Eater on the floor, the side of its skull smashed like a rotted pumpkin.

"The light, the light!" Kid screamed.

Sean couldn't bring himself to move. The Shadow Eater with the crushed skull twitched and sat up.

"Help!" Kid screamed.

Sean turned to find Kid on his back holding off an attack. Gripping both ends of his bat, Kid kept it between himself and a Shadow Eater's snapping jaws. Sean shone his light into the numb-muncher's eyes, making them sizzle. With a raspy shriek, it rolled from Kid and crawled into the darkness.

Kid leapt to his feet and snatched another flashlight from his tool belt. They ran. The escalator was near, Sean thought, they just might make it. Kid abruptly stopped by the open door of the storage room and Sean slammed into him.

"Oh, man," Kid muttered. His flashlight beam stopped on severed cables that stretched from the still-running generator. "How did they . . ."

"Hey, Kid," Sean said, near panic, "didn't you lock this door?"

Kid turned to look at Sean. Raw fear reflected on Kid's face. They ran toward the escalator but covered only a few yards, stumbling to a stop before a mass of bodies. A Shadow Eater about their age stood at the head of the group. In one hand, it held an ax. A key hung on a chain around its neck.

"The key to the lock," Kid said.

Sean noticed several compact discs looped by the chain. "It's Discman, isn't it?"

"Yeah."

"What are they doing?"

"I don't know. Ain't never seen 'em like this. I think we oughta—"

The ragtag army of dead bodies lumbered forward.

"Run!" Kid shouted, and they bolted, only to stop again as another mass of Shadow Eaters blocked them. Acting solely on instinct, Sean grabbed Kid by his shoulder, pulled him into the storage closet, and shut the door. Kid shut down the generator, and both boys pushed the heavy engine against the door just as the Shadow Eaters began banging on it. Kid jumped at a loud *ka-thunk*. "I don't believe it! They're using the ax."

"What are we gonna do?" Sean asked, his voice high and trembly.

"They're gettin' smarter," Kid said, turning to Sean. "Like— they're evolving."

"What?"

"The Shadow Eaters. The numb-munchers. They don't act like this. They're evolving, ya know, getting smarter. They ain't never used tools, but Discman used the ax to cut the cables. And the key! I can't believe it—he used the key to open the lock!"

"What do we do?"

"The ceiling!" Kid cried. "It's a drop ceiling. We go up and there's a crawl space. It'll take us anywhere in the basement!"

Splintering wood interrupted Kid's explanation. The head of the ax chopped through the door.

"Go!" Kid squatted in a corner and held his hands together for Sean to use as a step. Sean placed both hands on Kid's shoulders, put his foot in Kid's grip, and sprang up.

"The only thing that'll hold a body is crawling on the tops of the walls!" Kid shouted to him. "Don't crawl on the hung ceilings or you'll fall through like Joseph!"

Sean pushed aside a square of ceiling tile and pulled himself up. There was only about two and a half feet of space between the ceiling and floor above.

"Hurry, Sean! Help me up! They're almost through the door!"

Hearing the panic in Kid's voice, Sean spun on his perch and slammed his head against a vertical steel beam.

❧

When he woke, the batteries in his flashlight were dead. He sat up and felt the knot on the side of his head, wincing as he touched it. He peered down. The door was in pieces. Sean could make out the shape of the generator turned on its side. Kid wasn't in there.

He crawled in the direction of the escalator, lifted a ceiling tile, and saw the glint of metallic stairs directly below. He put his feet over the edge and wiggled down until he was hanging by his waist. From there he fell to the gray half-light on the escalator.

"Kid," he whispered, "Kid, are you down here?"

Something moved, but he didn't think it was Kid.

Outside, the buildings cast long shadows. He must've been unconscious for hours. He hurried; it would be dark soon.

The Twelfth-Floor Blockade didn't feel as safe as it once had. The one remaining generator hummed as it powered the lights in the fortress, the outer hallway, and down two flights of stairs. He went to the video display Kid had wired into six televisions. Six video cameras stood sentinel in the hallway and stairwell, showing him that all was well.

Sean lay on his cot in the Twelfth-Floor Blockade and thought about the small town he'd run away from. In all honesty, things hadn't been so bad with his parents. He'd begin the long trek home tomorrow.

⚜

"Did you break something?" Sean's mother yelled from a distant room.

"No, Mom, it's not me," he shouted back.

Wait a minute, he thought, *I'm not home. I'm at Kid's Twelfth-Floor Blockade.* He sat up. It had been a dream. He heard glass break from far away and jumped from his cot. Half of the televisions in the bank of screens were dark. He looked at the fourth monitor and could just see a shadowy group of people standing at a distance from the hall light. Something flew from them. One had thrown a brick at the lightbulb in the ceiling. The brick missed, but another was lobbed and he heard glass break. That camera turned the same black as the first three. Sean sat immobile as the two remaining lights in the hallway were extinguished.

A fist banged on the door, sounding like cannon fire. Kid had been right. They were getting smarter. They were evolving to the point of language. From the other side of the door came a raspy voice that he recognized.

"Sean, let us in—so hungry—open the—door—"

Ian Tremblin reached for the candle.

"Wait!"

"Wait for what, Wade? It is time to extinguish our final source of light."

"I can't do this. Not without light."

"Daemon Hall may allow you to leave after the tenth story—in the dark. You're just one step from completion and celebration."

"Celebration?"

"Your victory, Wade. You've won the contest. One more little story and you've won."

"At what cost?"

"Your fellow finalists would say it came at great cost." Ian Tremblin's face flared, then darkened as the candle burned to a stub. The flame sputtered. In the dying light, the writer revealed the dead gaze of Daemon Hall. "This house may yet own you. I may yet own you. Will it—will I consume you like the House on Butcher Ridge? Perhaps I will send forth an army of Shadow Eaters, your friends among them. Your undoing might come from your own head. What if human-size spiders ensnare you in their webs and eat you at their leisure?" The candlewick toppled, and the flame hissed out in melted wax. The writer's face faded to black.

I gripped my knees and gasped, "Mr. Tremblin?"

"Yes?" the horror master answered from the darkness directly behind me.

I turned in that direction. "What about the tenth story?"

"Yes, the tenth story." His voice now came from my right.

"Can we get on with it so I can leave? I feel like I might freak."

"Is insanity coming to call?" Ian Tremblin seemed to be walking around me, yet I heard no footsteps. *The last little finalist almost had it won.* I turned, trying to track his voice. *"Sadly, Wade went insane and then there were none."*

"Please, Mr. Tremblin," I begged.

"Please, Mr. Tremblin," the author said mockingly, circling faster, "please, Mr. Tremblin."

I stood and spun after Tremblin's scornful voice.

"Please, Mr. Tremblin—please, Mr. Tremblin—please, Mr. Tremblin—"

"STOP!" I cried, and fell to my knees, heart thundering. I couldn't draw a breath. "What—about the—tenth story?"

Ian Tremblin's voice came from every direction. "TONIGHT. THIS HOUSE. YOU."

"What? What do you mean?"

"ALL OF THIS: THE HOUSE, ME, AND MOST IMPOR-TANT, YOU, WADE. YOU ARE *IN* THE TENTH STORY."

The doors throughout Daemon Hall began to slam. Small creatures skittered in and ran across the floor. Things climbed down the walls, multiple limbs clattering. Shuffling footsteps approached from the hallway.

Ian Tremblin spoke once more. "Scary stories are great fun to read, but they're hell to live. And now that you know you're living in the tenth story, the question that remains is, will you make it out of the story alive?"

Epilogue

I shut the trunk on my brother's rust-red Volkswagen punch buggy. I have my license now, and he lets me borrow it from time to time. I climb behind the steering wheel and gaze blankly at the sparse dashboard. Sighing, I turn the ignition. The forty-year-old motor strains for several seconds before it catches. I look over at Kara in the passenger seat. Her face is as grim as mine feels. I shove the gearshift into first and drive from the gas station.

We ride along in silence. At least I have driving to distract me. Poor Kara, all she has to contend with are her fears. She opens the cavernous glove compartment and takes out the newspaper article encased in plastic. I'd shown it to her when I picked her up. I don't know why. I'm sure she read it when it was first published; for all I know, she has a copy of her own somewhere. It just seems important that we remember as much as possible.

Will Book Release Solve Mystery?

FROM STAFF

MAPLEWOOD—The death of a contest finalist has led to criminal charges against famed author Ian Tremblin. Why? Perhaps the answers will be forthcoming with the release of the new book *Daemon Hall*. The teenage author, Wade Reilly, is an eyewitness, yet he has not spoken of what occurred. According to doctors he has lost almost all ability to communicate. Since he was found wandering the grounds of Daemon Hall three months ago, he has been a patient at Morningside Mental Hospital.

Along with criminal charges, possible lawsuits could be brought on behalf of the parents of finalists. They claim the writer behaved in a negligent, harmful, and detrimental manner with regard to the safety of their children: Chelsea Flynt, Kara Bakshi, Demarius Keating, and Chris Collins, all residents of Maplewood. Each had entered a short story in a writing competition held by Ian Tremblin. As part of the contest they spent the night with the author in Daemon Hall. Flynt died from injuries received when she fell down the main staircase at the estate.

A statement released by Terence Bailey, Tremblin's lawyer, says, "My client was very upfront about the dangers involved in spending the night in what is documented to be a haunted house. In fact, prior to the contest night, all the finalists' parents signed waivers clearing my client of responsibility in the event of injury or death. We have learned that one finalist, Chris Collins, forged his father's signature, which, I feel, further negates any culpability on my client's part." Bailey's statement adds, "I would also like to point out that neither Wade Reilly nor his parents are taking part in any lawsuit. In fact, my client makes regular trips to see Wade at the hospital, visiting and editing Wade's book."

Doctors treating Wade Reilly say he has not spoken a word since he's been admitted. But according to Dr. Dwight Calhoun, chief resident at Morningside, "Wade has been writing feverishly since his first day here. It's almost as if he is trying to write that night out of his system. I believe that when he finishes the book, as he is close to accomplishing, he will speak again." Will the book reveal what really happened in Daemon Hall? "What Wade has written is what he believes occurred," Dr. Calhoun said. "I have read some of it. Frankly, it's a bit hard to swallow."

Reilly's book, *Daemon Hall*, is scheduled for release next year. ☐

Kara finishes the article. "When did you start talking agian?"

"When I put the last period at the end of the last sentence in the final chapter of the book." I glance at her and shrug. "Really, after that I could talk again." I turn onto the dirt road that leads to Daemon Hall. It's a fitting day to return. The sky is overcast with clouds like gray bands of iron. Perhaps a nighttime trip to the haunted house would be more appropriate, but that is something none of us will even remotely consider.

We round a curve, and there is the gate. Chris and Demarius turn in mute greeting as I pull beside Chris's brand-new Mustang Cobra. He'd gotten in a lot of trouble with his dad for coming to Daemon Hall that night. But his dad didn't hold a grudge, in light of the fact that Chris led his football team to the playoffs last season. Chris told me the car is his father's way of saying *Good job forgetting about all the artsy crap and concentrating on what really matters.* I shut off the VW; the engine rattles on awhile and then dies.

Kara and I get out and join the others at the fence. They have all changed over the past year. Both Chris and Demarius have grown taller, and Chris has packed on even more muscle mass. Kara is still the runt of the litter, but she no longer carries any baby fat. She is skinny, too skinny; her once plump cheeks are now sunken. She traded her glasses for contacts, exposing dark circles under her eyes. Of the four of us, I know that I have changed the most. Like Kara, I lost weight. The most outstanding

change, however, is my hair. In the fifteen weeks I was hospital-
ized, my hair turned completely white. Funny what terror will do
to a person.

Chris breaks the silence, being sensitive in his own unique
way. "Hiya, nut-job. Happy anniversary."

We laugh, enjoying the fleeting comfort it provides.

"It doesn't feel like a year has passed, does it?" Demarius asks.

"It seems like it happened last night," Kara answers.

"Even though it's been a year to the day," I add.

Chris looks carefully at me. "What did they diagnose you
with?"

"Severe anxiety disorder."

"What's that mean? You gonna go psycho and start killing
couples out at Lovers' Lane?"

"Nah, it's no big deal. I get panic attacks, that's all."

"A big enough deal that you got locked up for almost four
months," Demarius points out.

"That's where the *severe* part comes in. I had a bad attack,
and coupled with what went on, well, it sent me over the edge. It
was like a panic attack that lasted months. It was—horrible."

Full of nervous energy, Demarius climbs halfway up the gate
and looks through the bars at the mansion. "Are we sure we want
to do this?" he asks.

I nod. "My book comes out next month. You know what
might happen after that."

Demarius drops to the ground. "Yeah. Every teenage thrill-seeker from here to Timbuktu will come to see if there are really ghosts in there."

"And they'll learn there are," Kara whispers. "The worst possible kind."

"There's a more important reason we gotta do it," Chris growls.

No one speaks. Finally, Demarius says, "We don't know for sure that she's in there."

Chris grabs Demarius and pulls him to his side. With his free hand he points between the bars to Daemon Hall. "She's in there, and you know it. It took her spirit, her soul, and if we don't do something she'll be trapped forever."

Demarius pulls free. "Yeah. I know."

"I had forgotten how cool she was," Chris says. "It about blew me away when I showed up for the contest and there she was. I decided I was going to talk to her later, you know, privately. See if maybe I could get another chance." He pauses and wipes his eyes. "Anyway, if you were still in there, you know she'd be the first one trying to get you out."

We grow quiet, and like metal shavings, our attention is drawn by the magnetic pull of Daemon Hall. As we look at the mansion I think about what had happened to the others.

Chris mourns Chelsea, but for the most part he's the least affected. He had disappeared before most of the madness began. The only strange thing he remembers was when he'd gone to the bathroom that night. He heard someone whisper his name.

When his name was repeated, it sounded like the voice came from the drain in the sink. Then it was morning and he was waking up on the wet bathroom floor.

Demarius remembers standing on the diving board, followed by nightmares of drowning in cold black water. In the morning he was lying in the dry shallow end of the pool. Kara won't talk about what happened to her, but she showed up the next morning as they all silently gathered at Chelsea's body. They waited with Chelsea until police and rescue workers arrived, summoned by Ian Tremblin's driver.

Where was I during all this? I have no idea. By then my mind had shut down. They found me two hours later outside the house, aimlessly wandering the grounds.

I think about Chelsea, and how full of life she had been. I can't help but grin, remembering her description of how she'd leave Maplewood and rip off the rearview mirror before she'd even look back. I stop smiling. It turns out she's the one who can never leave. Then again, maybe we can fix that.

". . . doing this." Demarius is saying something to me.

"What?"

"I said, I can't believe you told Tremblin we'd be doing this," he repeats.

"He said that we're doing the right thing."

"Did it scare you the first time he showed up at the hospital?" Kara asks.

"Big time. And I almost didn't see him. My parents said no

way! They wanted him banned from the hospital. I'm surprised my dad didn't clobber him. But my doctor argued that it would help me, and in the end he convinced my parents to let Ian Tremblin visit. I was worried he was still the—the evil Ian Tremblin. He's not, and like the rest of you guys he can only remember that night up to a certain point. He remembers the mirror room and draws a big blank after that."

Chris looks mad. "If he thinks we're doing the right thing, why isn't he here with us?"

"He'd like to be here, I'm sure of it, but with all the legal problems he's had, it's better to keep a distance."

"Legal problems? That's an understatement," Demarius says with a laugh.

After our hellish night, Ian Tremblin's lawyer went right to work. The highly publicized case, in which he was charged with negligent homicide, lasted only two weeks. He was found not guilty, so Chelsea's father brought a civil suit against him. Before that case went to court, a cash settlement was made and the case was dropped. Afterward, Ian Tremblin's lawyer effectively squelched a lawsuit from Chris's and Kara's families.

"I didn't want my dad to sue him," Chris says. "But he was majorly pissed about the whole thing. Dad decided to drop it when he got to worrying that a lawsuit might screw up my football scholarship chances. I think Tremblin's lawyer was the one who put that bug in his ear."

"I didn't want my parents pursuing legal action either. All I want is to forget," Kara says.

We look through the gates for a few more minutes until Chris puts a hand on my shoulder. "Come on. Let's get this over with."

We walk to the cars and open our trunks. Chris pulls out a bolt cutter and passes it to Demarius. I grab the two five-gallon cans of gas I filled up at the gas station, and Chris gets another two from his trunk. Demarius uses the bolt cutter on the chain that secures the gate and takes one of the gas cans from me.

"Here," Kara says. She hands both Demarius and me a book of matches and slides a third into Chris's back pocket. "In case something grabs me again, I want you all to have matches. No matter what happens, we have to burn it."

We enter the gate, once again stepping onto Daemon Hall ground. We walk slowly, keeping abreast of one another.

"Are you sure this is going to work?" Demarius voices more doubts. "I mean, the house is made of stone."

"Which is why we have to go inside," Chris says grimly.

"The outer walls are stone, but inside it's different. The floors, ceiling, inner walls, and most of the furnishings are wood. It'll burn." I try to sound confident. "Worst that can happen is the outer shell remains standing, but at least we'll have torched Daemon Hall's black heart."

The rooftop gargoyles seem to turn their heads and watch us approach. An optical illusion, I tell myself. Doubts about our

success grow with each step. How powerful is Daemon Hall to have accomplished what it did? What chance do four scared teenagers have against it? Slowly, as I think about each worrisome concern, I fall back from the group. I finally stop altogether and look from dark window to dark window, wondering what awaits us inside. I think I see movement in a third-floor window, and I catch my breath. There! A figure looks down at us. It's surprising that I can see her at all because she's clothed totally in black. Except for a few strands radiating red like a hot flame, her hair, too, is black. Her skin had been pale when I'd known her in life. Now dead, her complexion is luminous. Chelsea smiles and raises a hand in greeting. I give a little wave.

"What are you grinning about?" Chris calls from the doorway.

He and the rest of the group watch me curiously. I look back to the third-floor window, but Chelsea is gone. Shrugging, no longer doubting, I join my friends at the front door.

Chris reaches for the doorknob. "Figures. It's open." He pushes the door wide. A familiar screech of hinges, a soundtrack to dozens of nightmares I'd had the past year, greets us.

"Do you really think we can pull this off?" Demarius asks.

Thinking of Chelsea in the window, I start to feel good, really good—better than I have in a year. "I'm positive," I answer. "Because this time we'll have help."

They all look at me oddly, waiting for an explanation. I simply smile and push past them.